A creature stepped out from behind a huge rock halfway up the steep slope. It banged its chest and roared.

Thud did such a good job that even the girls were startled. Being such a big kid, he filled out the gorilla costume impressively. In fact, in the low light of the ravine, you could hardly tell it was a gorilla outfit, which made it all the more impressive.

The kids screamed, of course, the girls as well as the boys.

The best part of this April Fool's joke, thought Lois, was that they could play it out for days and days. With luck, it could last the entire month of April.

THE HAMLET CHRONICLES SO FAR:

A Couple of April Fools

GREGORY MAGUIRE

HarperTrophy®
An Imprint of HarperCollins*Publishers*

For Judy Perlman and R. C. Binstock
and for Esther and Mahalia.

Also for Ann and Stona Fitch
and for Amelia and Claire.

Wise as sages, all—not an April fool among them!

A Couple of April Fools

Copyright © 2004 by Gregory Maguire

All rights reserved. No part of this book may be used or reproduced in any manner whatsoever without written permission except in the case of brief quotations embodied in critical articles and reviews. Printed in the United States of America. For information address HarperCollins Children's Books, a division of HarperCollins Publishers, 1350 Avenue of the Americas, New York, NY 10019.

Library of Congress Cataloging-in-Publication Data

Maguire, Gregory.

A couple of April fools / by Gregory Maguire.— 1st HarperTrophy ed.

  p.   cm. — (The Hamlet chronicles ; v. 6)

  Summary: At a Vermont elementary school, April Fool's Day takes on a sinister tone when a teacher goes missing and several suspects emerge, among them the teacher's fiance and a missing mutant chick.

  ISBN 0-06-076082-6 (pbk.)

  [1. April Fool's Day—Fiction.   2. Missing persons—Fiction.   3. Schools—Fiction. 4. Humorous stories.]   I. Title.   II. Series.

PZ7.M2762Co 2005   2004020847

[Fic]—dc22   CIP

                                                                   AC

Typography by Amy Ryan

❖

Originally published by Clarion Books, 2004
Published by arrangement with Houghton Mifflin Company
First Harper Trophy edition, 2005
Visit us on the World Wide Web!
www.harperchildrens.com

Moey eeny meeny miney.
Catch a dragon when he's tiny.
Moey miney eeny meeny.
Catch him while he's teeny-weeny.
Eeny meeny miney moe.
Snatch that dragon by the toe.
If he hollers . . . So? He hollers.
Sell him for a million dollars.

Contents

Happy Spring!

"**Y**ou don't look yourself this morning," said the farmwife to the mutant chicken. "That sprig of green feathers growing out of your scalp is a bit limp. Are you feeling all right, you mangy thing?"

The Vermont farmwife rattled spirals of seed corn into the yard. The improbable creature, looking hungry and dissatisfied, followed her around. To the east, over New Hampshire, a lilac dawn rinsed the sky. A rooster crowed across the valley. Somewhere a cow mooed in mild anxiety, waking its brethren, who lowed along.

The farmwife's boots made sucking noises in the barnyard mud. "Don't eat so fast, you spring fool; you'll choke."

She continued, mostly talking to herself. "But who's

a spring fool then? I'm old enough to be Moses' grand-mother, and an ordinary morning can still seem pretty enough to send shivers up my spine. It's the end of March, which, true to form even in contrary Vermont, has come in like a lion and shows signs of going out like a lamb. Mighty pretty."

The mutant chicken paid her no attention. It was gobbling seed so fast that it swallowed a largish pebble by mistake. The farmwife had to grab the creature and perform a modified Heimlich maneuver on it to clear its windpipe.

"I never gave emergency resuscitation to a chicken before," she admitted to herself. To the chicken, she added, "You may look like a chorus girl in a vaudeville number for an audience of turkeys, you silly thing, but you got a right to breathe, ain't you?"

She sniffed the air with sudden feeling. What's not to like on a spring morning in late March, when the wind freshens the barnyard, the bushes are notched with buds, and the black flies haven't come out yet? The farmwife took a moment to watch the mutant chicken go back to its breakfast. She took pity on the poor thing. It hadn't asked to be a mutant. It couldn't help that its genes had been spliced together, partly *Gallus domesticus,* partly blue-toe lizard. No more than she could help being closer to one hundred than to seventy-five.

"You're never too old to be a spring fool," she told herself. She wiped a little tear from one corner of her eye and promptly stepped in a huge mucky cowpie, and laughed at herself.

She turned to scrape her boot on a bit of fence rail. A movement in the thick of the forsythia fronds caught her eye. "Coydog?" she said, frowning. "Fisher cat? Not this time of day. Not this close to a human being."

"Old Man!" she called to her husband. "Bring the gun!"

She knew her husband was too deaf to hear her, but she hoped the stern sound of her voice would startle the creature in the bushes. It did. With a racket of thrashing bracken, a blurry commotion of claw and scale, the lurking visitor departed.

The farmwife walked over to investigate. Besides batons of broken forsythia, all that was left were a few bristles of hair and some cartilage from a chewed leg. As if a chipmunk had ended its life as someone's breakfast.

"You poor spring fool," she said aloud, though who could tell if she meant the dearly departed chipmunk, or its predator, or herself, having to witness the redness of tooth and claw that Nature can't help showing off once in a while.

1

The Wheel of Life

The teacher stood in a daze as two of her students thrashed and wrestled on the playground before her. Hair got yanked, arms got twisted. Punches were delivered. The tussling boys grunted in comic-book lingo: "Oof!" "Puuuh!" "Owwww!" "Grrr!" and the like. Around the edge of the scuffle, a dozen or so classmates shrieked. "Miss Earth! Help!" But the teacher appeared not to hear them.

"Miss Earth! They're killing each other! Blood will be shed!"

Miss Earth shook herself to attention. "Recess is over, children," she said. "Line up, please."

The boys detached themselves and brushed each other off. "Good job," murmured Sammy Grubb. His opponent, Thud Tweed, nodded briskly. They melted into the lineup. The other children in the class exchanged glances.

"Boys are such beasts," said Thekla Mustard, but halfheartedly. She knew the fight had been a fake. She had asked the boys to pretend to murder each other to see if Miss Earth would notice. These days, whenever Miss Earth was not actually teaching, her mind seemed to be on other things. But on what? Thekla couldn't tell. Was Miss Earth really engaged to Mayor Grass? If so, was she having second thoughts about the wedding? Adults were the most mysterious creatures on the planet.

If anyone could get to the bottom of Miss Earth's preoccupations, however, it was Thekla Mustard. Thekla, sometimes known as La Mustard, was Empress of the Tattletales, the girls' club in the classroom. Thekla had been its Empress since the dawn of time, which in this instance meant kindergarten. Thekla was *no-nonsense*. Thekla *ruled*.

The afternoon dragged on forever, weighed down by the task of converting fractions to decimals. Fawn Petros, for whom math was a puzzle, felt annoyed. Why bother to convert fractions to decimals? Why not let them live in peace, unconverted and companionable? Why did everything have to change into something else?

She sighed and shifted a decimal point several places

to see how it looked. Nice. Very nice.

"Fawn," said Miss Earth, peering over her shoulder, "you haven't really taken this in, have you? Look. Divide this by this, and presto! *Eureka!*"

"Divide who by which and *what?*"

"Eureka. A Greek phrase uttered by Archimedes when he had a brainstorm about the laws of the natural universe. It means: *Aha! I have found it! I have got it at last!*"

"Oh," said Fawn, who hadn't got it at all. "He got a fraction?"

"He got an idea. A solution. He had a brainstorm."

"That's nice for *him,*" said Fawn. "I only have a brain*fog.*"

"Don't worry," said Miss Earth. "Fogs clear in time. You'll get it. You can do it. Let's start over."

In the last few minutes of the day, Miss Earth relented. From a cardboard tube she unpacked a glossy educational poster. She taped it by its corners to the blackboard.

Shiny golden letters spelled out THE WHEEL OF LIFE. Smaller letters beneath that said LET US LIVE TOGETHER IN PEACE. Around the slogan stood a circle of animals holding hands or wingtips or touching whiskers. A cat and a dog were clasping paws. A lion nuzzled noses with a lamb. A single plankton rubbed its membranes against the quill of a porcupine.

Dubiously, Miss Earth said, "I think we got the kindergarten Science Fair poster by mistake."

Her students agreed. "The wheel of *life*?" asked Moshe Cohn, who prided himself on being the classroom's resident science whiz. "This looks like the wheel of ridiculousness."

"Miss Earth, don't animals tend to hate each other?" asked Anna Maria Mastrangelo.

"*Hate* is not the precise term, I think," said her teacher.

"Well," Anna Maria continued, "call it what you like, but my goldfish haven't spoken a word to each other in years."

"In the natural world, there is a concept of *predator* versus *prey*," began Miss Earth. "The eaters versus the eaten. Now, it's true that—"

"Did you know there's a clutch of baby alligators loose in the sewers of New York City?" interrupted Thud Tweed. Thud was a midyear transfer student, and he hadn't quite learned the classroom rules yet. "They swim up the plumbing into the toilet bowl and bite people on their bare bums."

"Surely not," said Miss Earth. "That's a plot from Stephanie Queen's celebrated novel *Mauled in Manhattan*. Now, class, settle down. Before we pack this poster off to the little kids, let's look at it seriously. Who can say what is incorrect about its message?"

Thekla Mustard observed, "This poster is no more than a sentimental invitation to interspecies dating."

"You're right, Thekla," said Miss Earth. "While living together in peace is a worthy goal, animals rarely demonstrate the goodwill that this poster shows. Let's send it to the kindergartners, and they can make what they like of it. A dartboard, maybe. Still," she went on, "the Wheel of Life is a valid notion in its own right. All living creatures share space on this planet. All creatures live in its light."

"Not alligators and crocodiles," said Thud Tweed. "They live in sewers, where there isn't any light."

"Don't distract me," said Miss Earth. "The annual Science Fair is approaching. The entire school is invited to participate. Children are expected to do displays, projects, or experiments on the theme of Our Natural World. The kindergartners will grow grass seed in milk cartons, I suppose. The lower school will do displays of flowers and pets. But our division is expected to consider the animal kingdom, creatures tame and wild. Tell me, what creatures might qualify as wild?"

"Bugs are wild," said Thud Tweed, pretending to groom himself under his arms and munch on what he found there.

"What about parakeets that were raised in cages but pecked their way through the bars to freedom?" asked Hector Yellow.

"Geese, ducks, pigeons?" said Fawn Petros.

"Pigeons aren't wild, they're just dumb," said Thud Tweed. "Like you."

Fawn glared and wished she could convert Thud from an overlarge bully into a fraction. A fraction of anything.

"Missing Links, like Bigfoot or Sasquatch, are wild," said Sammy Grubb. "So wild that no one is sure they even exist."

"Flameburpers are wild," said Salim Bannerjee sadly.

There was a silence. The class knew what he was talking about. A few weeks before, three genetically altered eggs had hatched nearby. The schoolkids had discovered that the emerging chicks were more than chicks. They seemed smart and cute. Since they knew how to breathe out little coils of fire, they had come to be known as *Flameburpers*. However, in the confusion that followed their discovery, one of the Flameburpers had met an untimely end. The second had disappeared into the woods, probably to become supper for some scavenger like a fox or a hawk. The third and last Flameburper was being raised by a stepchicken on Old Man Fingerpie's farm a mile or so out of town.

Miss Earth cleared her throat. "Domesticated animals can thrive living with humans or housed in a barn. Wild creatures often wither without their freedom. That's the distinction. Now, remember that since the genetic material of a Flameburper is part domestic hen and part Galápagos blue-toe lizard, we don't know whether a Flameburper will turn out to be wild or not. But in any case, we don't want to reveal its continued presence here in Hamlet, Vermont, do we? The press would descend and create unwanted havoc. So I propose that the last remaining Flameburper, tame or wild, be considered off-limits for this project. Are we agreed?"

All the children nodded except Salim, who was lost in a moment of grief. The Flameburper who had died had been in his care. Not quite a pet, not yet a friend, he—Seymour the Flameburper—had been a sort of kindred soul to Salim. Maybe, as a recent immigrant from Asia to Vermont, Salim had understood what being part-this-part-that might feel like for Seymour. In the Flameburper's case, not part-Hindu-part-Yankee, but part-chicken-part-lizard.

"Salim?" said Miss Earth gently.

Aha, thought Thekla, our teacher is not *completely* out to lunch. She can see that Salim is still upset about Seymour.

"Oh, yes, Miss Earth," said Salim politely. "I heartily

agree: None of us should take the remaining Flameburper as the subject of our project."

"Miss Earth," said Fawn Petros, "can an animal choose to be wild or tame? And can it be converted from one to the other, like decimals to fractions?"

Before Miss Earth could answer, Thekla Mustard bullied forward with her own thoughts, which she considered more important than Fawn's, or anyone else's for that matter. "Miss Earth," she said, "it is my firm opinion that *boys* are wild creatures. Did you see Sammy Grubb and Thud Tweed mixing it up on the playground earlier? Having a slugfest? Boys are hardly domesticated. Can we girls consider boys as a species of beast, and study *them*?"

The boys and girls actually had been getting along rather well since the sad affair of the Flameburpers, but Thekla was still trying to figure out the reason for Miss Earth's moody preoccupation. Poking a well-known sore spot usually worked.

"Boys will be boys," said Miss Earth, efficiently vague. "Technically they qualify as human beings, so let's be kind, shall we?"

"Well, why don't we sort ourselves into two teams to do these Science Fair projects?" suggested Thekla. "The girls versus the boys, as usual. The girls can constitute a Tattletale think tank."

More out of habit than anything else, Sammy Grubb murmured, "Or a Tattletale stink tank," but he didn't really mean it.

Miss Earth didn't nip these flippancies in the bud. Instead, she smartened her lipstick, peering at herself through the assignments written on the highly reflective surface of a whiteboard. She pursed her lips, making them full and gorgeous. "NO nastiness," she remarked over her shoulder, expecting sixteen *ooooooh-la-la*'s to blurt out behind her. But her students kept silent. Only the new kid, Thud Tweed, dared comment.

"Talk about *wildlife*," he said suggestively.

"Don't mind me," said Miss Earth. "I'm just going to New York for a screen test to audition for the role of that sizzling heroine Spangles O'Leary in the film version of *Mauled in Manhattan*."

"You *are*?" screeched Fawn Petros.

"I am not," said Miss Earth. "April Fool."

"It's not April for two more days!" protested Mike Saint Michael.

"Then I *really* gotcha, didn't I?" said Miss Earth. "Class dismissed."

Feeling rather foolish, Miss Earth's students walked in civilized single file out the door to the playground.

There, in the ordinary manner of schoolchildren on a warm spring day, they reverted to being wild goons and Godzillas. Thud Tweed leaped upon Sammy Grubb and pummeled him to the ground, in a happy-go-lucky, friendly sort of way. Who needs to find a Bigfoot or a Sasquatch with a Thud Tweed around, thought Sammy Grubb, from under $^2/_{25}$, or 8 percent, of a ton of Thud.

2

Trouble in Paradise?

The air was so nice that no one wanted to go straight home after school. Following an icy Vermont winter, spring seemed too good to waste behind the grimy windows of a school bus.

The girls began to draw hopscotch squares on the blacktop. The boys ambled along the roadside toward Grandma Earth's Baked Goods and Automobile Repair Shop.

"Did you have April Fool's Day in India, Salim?" asked Sammy Grubb. "April Fool's Day is when people try to fool each other. If you pull someone's leg successfully, you grin and poke them in the ribs and say, 'Haah haah, April Fool!' Because anyone who can be tricked so easily is an April fool."

"I know that," said Salim. "America is a place of

unfathomable customs, sometimes making India look like the Temple of True Reason. But in fact, April Fool's Day is popular in India too."

"Do they have Bigfoots in India?" asked Sammy Grubb. "Or do I mean Bigfeet?"

"Up in the Himalayas, I think. They're called yetis."

"Bigfoot, Bigfeet, Bigbunions: Give it a rest, Sammy," said Thud, interrupting. "Now, look, guys. I'm still the new kid on the block. I have a question. You boys in Miss Earth's class are always trying to prove that boys are cleverer than girls. Do we try to make April fools of the girls in Miss Earth's class? Those so-called Tattletales?"

Everyone glanced at Sammy Grubb. He was the Chief of the Copycats, the club of boys that stood as loyal opposition to the Tattletales. Before Sammy could form a reply, however, they had reached the shop. They all piled in. The smell of powdered sugar and diesel oil spillage was intoxicating.

Grandma Earth, their teacher's mother, was looking beleaguered behind the counter. "Hello, lads," she said. "Where's my daughter when I need her? Is she doing detention duty because one of your number misbehaved? I'm having a hard time keeping up with the kitchen work around here, what with everyone wanting a spring tuneup."

"Don't know," said Sammy. "Doesn't she go to see Mayor Grass when she gets out of school?"

"Your guess is as good as mine. Love is great for those in love and a pain in the neck for everyone else," said Grandma Earth. "Make up your minds. What'll it be, boys?"

The Copycats stocked up on doughnuts and went back outside.

His thinking improved by a rush of sugar, Sammy said, "You know, everybody got in a whole lot of trouble when we Copycats and Tattletales squared off during the annual Spring Egg Hunt. Maybe for once we should give the old *us-them* thing a rest."

The boys weren't used to this sort of approach from Sammy Grubb. "Losing your nerve in battle?" said Thud Tweed.

"Oh, everything's not a battle," said Sammy mildly. "I guess we can learn from our mistakes, can't we?"

Nobody wanted to admit that boys ever made mistakes, so there was a lot of heavy-duty doughnut chewing instead.

"Anyway," said Sammy decisively, "the girls will be expecting us to play a big April Fool's Day joke on them. So if we don't, they'll be jumpy and nervous all day long waiting for it. We can agitate them without even trying."

"That's more like it," said Mike Saint Michael. "You

think like a chief, Chief."

No one noticed the little gleam in Thud Tweed's eye. Thud was too new a member of this class to be bored by the same things that bored them. He thought a little April Fool's joke sounded like a good idea. A harmless prank—why not? Stir things up a bit. And if the boys wouldn't join in—well, he could look for collaborators elsewhere.

The girls in the Tattletales Club weren't interested in hopscotch. That was a ruse. They had another agenda.

They were waiting for Miss Earth to emerge from school. Dolled up in her lipstick and eyeliner, would she hop aboard her Kawasaki 8000 Silver Eagle motorcycle and hurry home to grade papers? Or did she have a more romantic plan? Would her beau, Mayor Grass, swing by in the town dump truck and pick her up? Listlessly, the girls hopped and scotched, waiting to find out.

The school secretary, Mrs. Cobble, hobbled out. She supported the small of her back with one hand. Being a school secretary was hard work. She maneuvered herself into her station wagon and drove off.

Here came Nurse Pinky Crisp, her stethoscope flapping on her bosom like a snake on a trampoline. She jumped into her fin-hipped vintage '57 Ford and roared away.

Janitor Jasper Stripe emptied some trash baskets, and a few candy wrappers blew away in the wind. Thekla Mustard, who believed Nature should be Clean as well as Beautiful, scowled but kept her thoughts to herself.

Finally their wait was rewarded. Out came Miss Earth, looking like a million bucks. Her hair was held back with a barrette shaped like a red squirrel. Her ears were adorned with small blue plastic butterflies. Her shoulders were covered with a black-fringed shawl printed with yellow grosbeaks. You'd guess that the lace on the hem of her skirt had been spun by exceptionally capable spiders. She was a walking exhibit of Our Woodland Friends—or a running exhibit. She was moving at a clip.

Beside her stomped Ms. Frazzle, the kindergarten teacher, in green knee-high rubber boots. "You look worried, Germaine," she said to her colleague. "Everything okay in Loveland?"

Miss Earth readied her motorcycle ignition key. "Oh, the wedding plans aren't going well," she murmured, as if she didn't want to take the time to discuss it just now.

"There's always a hitch or two in getting hitched," said Ms. Frazzle kindly, encouragingly.

Miss Earth glanced at her watch. "Silly me, I'm almost late," she said. "There'll be trouble in Paradise if I stand my fellow up." She wiggled her fingers goodbye.

Her diamond ring sparkled. Then she sped off on her motorcycle.

The girls were disappointed that Mayor Grass hadn't come by. They wanted to see lip-smacking romance up close and personal. But at least they'd confirmed once and for all—Eureka!—that Miss Earth was engaged. That diamond was an *engagement* rock. The hopscotch game petered out as the girls discussed the news.

"I wonder if we'll be invited to the wedding this summer?" said Thekla Mustard. "Do you think Miss Earth will need seven bridesmaids? If so, I'll be Boss Bridesmaid."

"Why should you?" said Lois Kennedy the Third, kicking a stone. "Just because you're Empress of the Tattletales doesn't mean you get to be chief cheese on every deli platter."

"Glory follows glory, in my experience," explained Thekla. "You wouldn't know glory if it woke you up with a trumpet blast. Now don't distract me; I have an idea. Girls, friends, minions: let's go visit the Flameburper at Old Man Fingerpie's farm."

Why not? It was a class act of a late March afternoon. So the Tattletales made their way up the hill along Squished Toad Road. In sunnier patches of roadside, the spring's first ferns were uncurling their fiddleheads.

"What did Ms. Frazzle mean, 'Everything okay in

Loveland?'" asked Fawn Petros.

"She meant were Miss Earth and Mayor Grass still getting along like lovebirds," explained Carly Garfunkel, who took a great interest in romantic matters in case they ever mattered to her.

"Rather than getting along like, say, Siberian snow spiders?" asked Fawn. "Or penguins, or mules?"

"Of course they're getting along like lovebirds!" said Sharday Wren. "Anyone with eyes in her skull can see that."

"Why hasn't Miss Earth announced her wedding plans to us, though?" asked Nina Bueno. "Could it be she's having second thoughts?"

A small cloud wandered in front of the sun and made several girls shiver at once. "Nonsense," said Lois Kennedy firmly. "Once in love, always in love. You *never* escape from love. It keeps you in its clutches *forever*."

The way Lois put it, love sounded less like a big fat bonus and more like a fatal medical condition. For a minute, the girls were glad to be too young for serious romantic combat.

3

Dreamboat or Dump Truck?

Flossie Fingerpie was repairing the barn roof with a bucket of tar. She brandished her brush at the girls as they passed beneath her into the cool, pleasant stink of the dark barn.

A few cows nodded courteously. The stepchicken, a scatterbrained hen named Doozy Dorking, raced forward to greet the visitors and ran smack into a post. You could almost see the little stars wheeling around her head as she thought to herself, Wha—wha—where am I? When she regained her balance, she began to run again.

The Flameburper followed. The kids had been visiting it several times a week, and every time they looked in, it had changed some more.

Today they noticed that the Flameburper's neck was

elongating. Its body looked less like a dumpling and more like the sack of a deflated bagpipe. The little green feathers on top weren't so airy anymore. They were straightening up into a rack of feathery quills that began at the forehead and ran across the skull back toward the spine. The feathers fell forward with a soft *plosh,* like a lady's fan closing. Then they opened again.

"It's a curious varmint, all right," said Old Man Fingerpie, coming into the barn with a tin bucket of mash. "Bet it's gonna be bigger than its stepmother."

"But which one is it?" said Thekla for the thousandth time.

It was a puzzle. Three creatures had hatched out of the weird eggs. At first called A, B, and C, they had come to be known as Amos, Beatrice, and Seymour. When Seymour had died, the remaining two had gotten mixed up. One had disappeared and the other hadn't. Was the Flameburper at Fingerpie Farm bellicose Amos, or was it fun-loving Beatrice? If it was Beatrice, she didn't look fun-loving anymore. But then, one of her siblings had recently died, and the other was missing and presumed dead. So whoever this one was, Amos or Beatrice, he or she might be depressed about the death.

"Don't you remember the way to tell?" said Old Man Fingerpie. "Pick it up by its legs. If it cranes its neck and pecks your fingers, it's a male. The females can't do that."

None of the girls wanted to try. With its flexible neck, the Flameburper looked far too capable of pecking. But Old Man Fingerpie wasn't scared of Nature in any form, even biotech accidents. He snatched the Flameburper and held it upside down. It squirmed and writhed, but it couldn't peck his hands, however it tried.

"Beatrice!" the girls cried with renewed affection.

Lois Kennedy the Third, who had taken Beatrice into her own special care, tried to snatch up the Flameburper for a snuggle. But Beatrice appeared not to want any snuggling just now. She burped out a tiny warning flame, keeping Lois away.

"So much for your basic animal magnetism," said Old Man Fingerpie, putting a clothespin on his nose. "See you later, ladies. I'm gonna muck out the pigpen." Out he clomped toward the smelliest building on the property, a good way downwind of the house.

The girls watched Doozy and Beatrice. Lois threw a bit of seed corn their way. Doozy plunged forward, intending to claim the morsel by rights of seniority. But Beatrice intercepted the pass with a clever swipe by an upper claw.

Upper claw? Chicks don't have upper claws.

"Oh my goodness, look!" said Lois. She tossed another piece of corn. "Here, Beatrice. Here, girl. Get this one."

Beatrice danced forward. Instead of craning her neck, as her stepmother would have done, she reared her neck back and lifted her scrawny wings. Jointed limbs unfolded from beneath them. They were orange, like her legs. They flexed forward, and their eensy claws cupped together. Beatrice caught the seed and fed herself.

"Yet another message from the universe: Nature is tricky," said Thekla. "This Flameburper is exhibiting her blue-toe lizard DNA. That's a lizardy kind of claw she's tucked under that wing of hers."

"Good girl!" shouted Lois. "Look how you're growing, a little bit every day!"

Lois's elation, perhaps, was babysitter's pride. The other Tattletales felt a bit squeamish. "A hen with hands?" said Nina Bueno dubiously. "Kind of freaks me out."

"Of course," said Carly Garfunkel. "The Flameburper *is* a freak."

"What's she going to develop next?" said Anna Maria Mastrangelo. "Dalmatian spots and a hundred centipede legs?"

"She could develop the fangs of a vampire," said Lois staunchly. "I'd still love her. Now look: Wouldn't it be great if we could somehow use her new talents in some April Fool's trick on the boys?"

"I was going to bring up that subject," said Thekla.

"I'm not sure we ought to engage in that kind of cheap competition anymore. Haven't we learned anything these past few months?"

"But right now's the perfect time for a kicker," said Lois. "Just when the boys will think we've gotten complacent."

"Miss Earth encouraged us not to draw attention to the existence of a Flameburper in our midst," said Thekla. "Leave it alone, Lois. Let it go."

"Maybe you don't want to lead the charge, Thekla, because you're worn out. You need a holiday, if not a rest cure. Why don't you resign and let some new blood get elected? Like, say, *me*?"

"You can't be in charge. You don't know how to be Empress of the Tattletales. You're not trained."

"What Ivy League school did *you* attend to qualify?" asked Lois.

"Consider the matter dropped," said Thekla. "No April Fool's trick on the boys. And no parading the Flameburper about, claws or no. Now listen up, girls. I'm concerned about what Miss Earth said. Do you really think there's trouble in Paradise? Shouldn't we go into high-alert spy mode and snoop around a bit? Maybe in our humble little way, we could help."

"How could there be trouble?" asked Anna Maria Mastrangelo. "Mayor Tim Grass is a regular dreamboat."

"Nah, he's nice enough, but he's not a dreamboat," said Sharday Wren. "He's a very okay dump truck, that's all."

"We have no proof that anything is wrong," said Anna Maria.

"Miss Earth said things weren't going well," said Fawn. "What does that mean?"

No one was sure. But before they could discuss it, Beatrice the Flameburper began to glance around with a curious, alarmed expression. Her little claws came out from beneath her wings. If they hadn't known any better, they would have thought Beatrice was wringing her claws in worry.

The girls backed up and forgot the business about the happiness of Miss Earth and Timothy Grass.

"Shouldn't somebody call a vet?" asked Sharday. "That bird don't look at all healthy to me."

Flossie Fingerpie was peering in the open door. "It's my belief that something out there is spooking her," she said. "I flushed some sort of a varmint from the property this morning, and that silly young critter has been agitated ever since."

"We figured out who this is. It's Beatrice," said Lois.

"If my old tired eyes aren't tricking me and Beatrice is developing hands, maybe she can start helping out with the chores," said Flossie Fingerpie.

"What can we do to calm her down, though?" asked Lois.

"Go away, and close the door behind you," said the farmwife. "If she thinks something is out to get her, closing her in will make her feel safer. And *be* safer too," she added. "We wouldn't want anything to happen to our last remaining freak of Nature, would we?"

4

Grownups in Their Natural Habitat

The sun shimmered and splashed through the budding silver maples that lined both sides of Squished Toad Road. When it wasn't freaking out, Nature was sprigged with good humor.

Well, that's what Thekla Mustard was thinking, anyway, as she left the other Tattletales and began to head down the hill toward her home.

Thekla Mustard was having an interesting year. She had begun it, as she'd begun every year since first grade, full of enthusiasm for leadership. She led by inspiration or by intimidation, whichever worked best at the moment. She liked being Empress of the Tattletales, a role she had held since she had thought it up.

But Thekla could tell there was a leadership crisis brewing. She knew that Lois Kennedy the Third had

had her eyes on the prize for some months now. Thekla could sense a challenge in the offing.

The anticipation of a good fight made the spring seem all the more tender and lovely. The birds at their afternoon exercises, the llamas at Cormiers' farm doing a fine prance. The forsythia wands leaning over the electrified fence were serrated with furled buds promising yellow sooner or later. Any day now, rabbits and woodchucks would be squabbling over the same garden lettuces. The world could be so sweet sometimes.

As she cut her way along the back of Cormiers' farm, heading for the woodsy end of Sugar Maple Road, Thekla spotted Miss Earth's motorcycle. It was parked next to the town dump truck. The two vehicles were almost nuzzling nose to nose under a white pine tree. And overlooking Foggy Hollow, on an embankment already shin-high with first-growth meadow, stood Miss Earth and Mayor Timothy Grass. They were standing near enough to hold hands, but they were not holding hands.

Hmmm, thought Thekla. It may well be that no one else is as interested in these romantic developments as I am. But here's a chance to observe the wild grownup in its natural habitat. Another sort of animal magnetism, she supposed. I wonder how close I can get.

It's not really spying, she said to herself as she sank to her knees and began to snake herself through the conveniently tall grasses. This field is public property. Anyone who feels like slithering about is totally allowed.

A helpful wind soughed through the trees, disguising the sound of her approach. She drew as near as she dared. The problem was that if she was near enough to hear over the sound of the wind, she was too near to raise her head and look. They'd see her head like a helium balloon bobbing at knee height. She'd never get away with it. So she crawled and wriggled to within a few feet of the lovebirds, closed her eyes, and listened.

"Are you having second thoughts, Tim?" said Miss Earth in a rather neutral tone.

Mayor Grass didn't answer for a moment. "I wonder if *you're* having second thoughts," he said at last.

"All thoughts are second thoughts, following the One Big Thought," she said, sounding just a tiny bit like the teacher she was. "I like the notion well enough, of course. But I'm interested in this tenor."

"Tell me about him," he said.

"He's pretty impressive," she admitted. "But he may be unavailable."

"Germaine, I want you to be happy. . . ."

"But how can I know what I want?"

"Whatever you want is fine with me. I'll deal."

Thekla couldn't believe her ears. On the very day she'd finally had proof of the engagement of the first selectman of Hamlet, Mayor Timothy Grass, to Miss Germaine Earth, teacher extraordinaire, the romance was taking a nosedive toward oblivion! It was on a one-way trip to Nowheresville! It was becoming History!

"You sound upset," said Miss Earth.

"I've got my mind on lots of other things," he said. "There's the annual town meeting coming up. The budget committee is up in arms over our insurance premiums. And I'm trying to make sure the new fire engine is ready for delivery before the Fourth of July so we can show it off in the parade. Don't worry about me."

"I do worry about you," she said. "I can't help it."

"I can look after myself," he said, and then added, "when I need to."

Thekla imagined she could hear the sound of two hands gripping each other, but maybe it wasn't Miss Earth holding Mayor Grass's hand. Maybe it was Miss Earth's own two hands wringing each other in distress.

There was the sound of a little light lip suction. Thekla didn't know enough about kisses to categorize them, but this kiss seemed dry and cousinly to the ear. Was it the Big Kiss-Off?

"Mother will be wondering where I am," said Miss Earth. She sounded sad.

"I'll always remember you like this," said Mayor Grass. "Don't leave me."

"I have to. I have to go," said Miss Earth. And off she went. Luckily she was looking back at Mayor Grass, so she didn't see Thekla Mustard when she stepped on her hand.

Thekla grimaced into the grasses to keep from crying out. Her tears of pain, though real, quickly became tears of sorrow for Tim and Germaine. (Suddenly she was thinking of them as Tim and Germaine.) What had she just heard? It was so confusing. What was this about a tenor? What choice was Miss Earth struggling with? And Mayor Grass so tolerant, so attentive, so loving. So mayoral.

She heard the rich throaty purr of the Kawasaki 8000 Silver Eagle motorcycle as Miss Earth left her boyfriend in the dust. Eventually the old dump truck followed at a more stately, arthritic pace.

Thekla sat up and looked around. The world didn't look so beautiful anymore. Oh sure, the sun was still dancing through the tops of the trees; the meadow was hung with a sudden smudge of midges that had hatched a few moments earlier and would be dead within the hour. The distant sound of traffic from Interstate 89 still whooshed in its daily recital. But somewhere two grownups were going their separate ways. For a day or forever?

It was mysterious. The world could break your heart sometimes.

In the drier months, the path through Foggy Hollow was a shortcut, but in the muddy slop of spring, progress would be slow. So Thekla made her way down Sugar Maple Road and turned the corner by the library. There she came across the rest of the Tattletales again.

Though Thekla was eager to tell her subordinates what had happened, she paused a minute. She didn't like seeing the girls together without her. Sure, it was a free country, and the Bill of Rights guaranteed the right of free assembly. But Thekla was an *empress,* and the Founding Fathers surely couldn't have meant that schoolgirls had the right to convene without her supervision.

Before Thekla could speak, Lois Kennedy the Third explained. "We came back from Fingerpie Farm to look up blue-toe lizards in the library."

"What for?"

"That Beatrice looks seriously overwrought to me," said Sharday. "She's jumping and thrashing like she thinks there's a boa constrictor nearby. A boa with a yen for a Flameburper sandwich. We know what preys on chickens. Foxes, mostly. But what preys on lizards? We got curious. But we got here too late. The library is closed."

"I'll dispatch a library research crew tomorrow," said Thekla briskly. "Bigger news now. Pay attention, girls. My hunch was right. Or I should say, Miss Earth was right to be worried. There's trouble in Paradise."

"You're not on about that again?" said Lois. "We've got an April Fool's prank to plan and a nutty Flameburper to calm down, and you're still zeroing in on hearts and flowers?"

"Hearts and *daggers*," said Thekla suggestively, but no one rose to the bait.

"You're preaching to a congregation of one. Yourself. Who cares about hearts?" asked Lois. "Nobody wants to give up on a chance to put one over on those Copycats. You're losing the pulse, Thekla. You haven't got the goods to be Empress anymore."

"So? What are you saying? *Lois?*"

"If I were voted Empress, I could *be* Empress, Thekla. You know it. I'd learn on the job. I'd do as good a job as you, if not better."

"Oh, come off it. Who would ever even nominate you?" said Thekla. "Look, even if *I* nominated you, no one would vote for you."

"If you're so sure, why don't you try it?" said Lois. "Go ahead. I dare you."

Thekla paused just an instant too long. "Okay. I will." In a bored voice, she continued: "I call for a vote.

34

I nominate Lois Kennedy the Third to take over as Empress of the Tattletales."

"I second it," said Lois.

"Motion seconded. Let's vote. Hands, girls. Who votes for Lois?" Thekla put her own hand up and smirked. "So you get one vote, Lois. Maybe you'll vote for yourself too. Two to five. The election is over."

Lois did vote for herself.

The other girls looked at Thekla. Her chin was up and her hand was up. What were they supposed to do? If their leader was voting for Lois, maybe they should follow suit. Carly's hand went up, and so did Sharday's. Nina's hand went up. Anna Maria shrugged and put her hand up. Fawn pretended to scratch her head, raised her hand briefly, scratched her head again, and buried both her hands in her armpits.

"Seven to nothing. It's a landslide," said Lois.

"Recount! I demand a recount!" shouted Thekla. "It was coercion! It was fraud! I demand a recount! Who seconds my demand?"

Nobody seconded.

Lois smiled. Her dream had come true. For the first time since kindergarten, Thekla Mustard had been deposed. Legally, and probably only temporarily, but deposed just the same.

"Empress Lois," she said dreamily. Then she sat up.

"All right, girls. To business. What'll we do to the Copycats *this* time?"

Thekla, still stiff from her moments in the meadow, her hand still throbbing from where Miss Earth had stepped on it, backed away. She spoke in a voice as basso profundo as she could manage. "*Oh. My. God*. I have created a monster."

But nobody paid her any attention.

5

The Mustard Motto

"You're late, Thekla," said her mother. "Look at the time."

"I was held up with meetings," said Thekla, tossing her backpack in a heap in the corner.

Thekla was nothing if not orderly; Mrs. Mustard raised an eyebrow. But she only said, "Wash your hands, dear. I'm about to serve dinner."

"My hands are clean, like my conscience," said Thekla. But she ran water over her hands quickly and took her seat.

The room was sunk in its customary Old World gloom. Dr. Mustard had already taken his place at the head of the table. His antique pince-nez were perched on the tip of his elegant nose. The light from an oil lamp with an amber glass globe made Josif Mustard's face look warm and kindly, though it was also deeply shadowed with wrinkles. *He* was no spring chicken—he was old enough to be Thekla's grandfather.

"Ah, my daughter," he said, and nodded his head in greeting as if she were a delegate at a convention. He rose slightly from his chair.

"Good evening, Father," said Thekla. She removed the damask napkin from its silver ring. "How was your day?"

Thekla's father was an eye doctor who made eyeglasses too. But the work was wearing, and his own eyesight was none too good anymore. He sighed and said, "I gave an exam today to Widow Wendell. She wants new tinted contact lenses to match the color of her newly tinted hair. But when I squinted to follow her recitation of the eye chart, the letters seemed to spell out a message in Polish."

Mrs. Mustard set out the dumplings wrapped in cabbage leaves, the kielbasa in cloves and mustard seed, the potatoes boiled in their skins and draped with translucent rings of Vidalia onion. "What did the message say?" she asked her husband.

"It said, *Uwazaj co wybierasz.*"

"What does it mean, Josif?" asked Mrs. Mustard. She took her seat and set her napkin in her lap.

When his wife was ready, Dr. Mustard raised a glass

of muscatel and said, "*Uwazaj co wybierasz* means *Beware what you choose*. It is something my dear mother used to say in my youth. I suppose I must be feeling old. It is almost as if my dear mother were speaking to me, saying: Choose carefully, Josif. Life is brief, and when it's done, it's done."

Thekla grasped her glass of good pasteurized Vermont milk for the evening toast. Her mother lifted a beaker of soda water. The Mustard family loved ritual and did everything every day in the same way.

"To God, who breathes life into us; to the memory of my mother, who sacrificed so much for me; to my family, a comfort and a consolation; and to nearsightedness, the correction of which puts bread, butter, and kielbasa upon our table."

They drank. "Don't gulp, Thekla dear," said Mrs. Mustard.

"Why did you think your mother wanted to speak to you?" asked Thekla. "And through an eye chart, of all things? Sounds spooky to me."

Dr. Mustard looked up. At the end of the dining room, on the wall behind his wife's chair, where he could see it every evening, hung a larger-than-life-size portrait of Grandmother Thekla Mustard. She had been a well-cushioned woman, and her high-necked blouse was a golden silk slope against which rested several strings of pearls. She looked like a baroness of some sort. Piled in big loops upon the cliff face of her forehead, her hair looked like several dozen balls of gray angora wool. In real life she hadn't worn silk or pearls; the portrait painter had invented for her a luxury she'd never known.

"My sainted mother," said Dr. Mustard, "seemed to be saying, *Josif, don't be fooled by the exuberance of springtime. Death will come even to you, so pay attention. Beware what you choose.*"

"But what is there to *beware*?" asked Mrs. Mustard. "Are you thinking of taking up skydiving at your age, Josif? Please don't. Your bad knee, remember." She was only kidding, trying to cheer her husband up.

"The point is that one must make every moment in life count, Norma Jean," he answered. "My poor mother, of excellent character though unfortunately a pauper, emigrated from Poland just as the Second World War was flaring up. She brought nothing to America but her good name, seventy dollars sewn into her undergarments, her husband, and a will to succeed."

Thekla had heard this story many times before. She rolled her eyes. Her mother flashed her a look— *Behave*—and then said, "Mustard. Is that such a good name in Poland?"

"In Poland the family was called Mustowelowski,"

said Dr. Mustard. "As my mother stood in line at Immigration, nearly fainting from hunger, my father bought her a frankfurter on a bun. She didn't like eating in public, considering it unseemly. But she didn't want to faint from hunger during her interview. So she ate as quickly and discreetly as she could. When she and my father had their interview, the agent noticed that one line of the application was smudged with a yellow stain. 'What's that?' he asked, pointing to their last name. 'Mustard,' said my mother, proud that she knew the word in English. On the strength of her language skills, the pair of them were admitted, but the immigration agent thought their family name was Mustard and wrote it in their visas. And so it has been ever since."

Thekla knew that her grandmother had been a wonderful woman. Following the death of her husband by flu, she had raised her only child, Josif, to be a good son, a good eye doctor, and a good citizen. To put him through medical school, she had scrubbed floors and emptied ashtrays on all 102 floors of the Empire State Building. She had lived just long enough to be fitted with a pair of eyeglasses—her son's first pair. She had put them on and cried, "*Voilà!* I see the world anew!" Then she had died of happiness. She had been buried with her new glasses on.

"Josif, why do you think your mother is speaking to you from beyond the grave?" asked Mrs. Mustard. "That's not like her."

"Life flies on wings," he answered. "We must do what we love before it is too late. Thekla, my dear, what do you love most to do?"

Boss the Tattletales, thought Thekla sourly. But she supplied a more acceptable answer. "Homework," she said.

"Then you should do as much homework as possible, with *gusto*!" said her father.

"But what do you love most, Josif?" said his wife.

"I love eyes," he said. He took off his little glasses, which flexed smartly thanks to a little hinge in the nosepiece. He stared at himself in the convex surfaces of the lenses. Then he replaced the spectacles and looked over the head of his wife at his mother's eyes. "I love eyes," he repeated. "I love to see and to help people see." But he blinked, as if not trusting his tired old eyes to see as well as they once had.

Mrs. Mustard stared down at her cabbage leaves as if she thought that her own eyes were not worth staring into. Thekla felt a little sorry for her.

"What do you love most, Mother?" she asked.

"Why, my family, of course," she answered, perhaps a little too quickly.

"And what next?" Thekla persisted.

"Keeping my mouth shut so I can hear others speak," Mrs. Mustard said, with a wry little grin. "You tell me about *your* day, Thekla."

Thekla did not want to talk about her day. She had lost control of the Tattletales for the first time since the club was founded in kindergarten. What would strong Grandmother Thekla have done in such a situation? Immigrated to a new country?

"Thekla," said Dr. Mustard in a soft voice, "your mother asked you a question. Do not fail to answer her."

"Yes, of course, Father," said Thekla immediately. "My day was filled with good solid book learning and profitable exercise in the open air, and I was stabbed in the back by my traitorous friends, may they all roast in—"

"Thekla!" The pince-nez dropped into her father's napkin. "Was someone unkind to my little princess?"

"*Unkind* doesn't begin to cover it," said Thekla.

"Tell us, Thekla." Mrs. Mustard leaned forward. "We should know."

"I have been—I have been *ousted* from my position as Empress of the Tattletales!" If Thekla hadn't been so angry, she might have burst into tears. But the expression of Grandmother Thekla on the wall seemed to communicate another family motto: *Tears are a waste of time.*

"That's unthinkable!" said Dr. Mustard. "You founded the society of Tattletales! How can they possibly proceed without you at their head?"

"It's not so unthinkable," said Mrs. Mustard. "Perhaps it's not even all that unfortunate, Thekla. Being a solo agent has its advantages."

"What are you going to do, Thekla?" asked Dr. Mustard.

"What *are* you going to do?" repeated his wife.

Thekla didn't know. She shrugged and helped herself to a little mustard for her kielbasa. "Bide my time," she said at last.

Dr. Mustard sat up a little straighter. He seemed relieved. "Maybe that's why Grandmother Mustard seemed to be communicating with me today. So I could remind you: You always have a choice. Just beware what you choose. You've lost your position, but you can choose to fight for what's yours. You have a right to it. Did Grandmother Mustard ever take a setback lying down? She did not. Were I you, I would fight to reclaim my rightful position. That's what I would choose to do."

Mrs. Mustard smiled a bit wanly. She said nothing, and her silence seemed to suggest: *Were I you, I would choose to lie down and play dead. It's not such a bad strategy. Take it from me.*

"All things change," said Thekla sadly. "I'm not Empress anymore. I wonder if private life might be in any way rewarding?"

Over Thekla's shoulder, Grandmother Mustard scowled through the varnished layers of the past. She seemed to be thinking, No granddaughter of mine gets deposed without putting up a fight, or she's not a very saucy Mustard.

6

Scheming and Not Scheming

The next day, Thursday, was the last day of March. "It's not April Fool's Day until tomorrow," said Miss Earth. "No tricks today, kiddos."

At recess, the children separated into their usual klatches. The Tattletales gathered near the hopscotch squares on the blacktop. The Copycats lurked near the basketball hoop. Pearl Hotchkiss, the only child in Miss Earth's class who refused to belong to a club, sat on a step and read a big fat Harry Potter book.

"Emergency meeting of the Tattletales," said Lois Kennedy the Third. "Tomorrow is April Fool's Day. We have to work fast if we're going to trick the boys. I have the start of a plan—"

"Just a start?" said Thekla. "I always announced my plans in perfect finished form."

"Did you ask for permission to speak?" replied Lois.

"Free speech is promised me by the Bill of Rights," said Thekla hotly.

"I'm Empress. I make the rules," said Lois. "Okay: Speak."

Thekla smacked her lips shut. She folded her arms.

"Here's one idea," continued Lois. "The cement mixer's on-site today because the new pavement is being poured for the sidewalk out back. I wonder if we could ask one of the workers to dump a spare load of wet cement somewhere in Foggy Hollow, and maybe we could chase the boys into it and trap them there."

"And then what?" said Nina. "Leave them to die with their socks full of cement?"

"Oh, just laugh a lot, and then dial 911," said Lois.

"That's too mean," said Carly, and the other girls agreed.

"Well," said Lois, "whatever we decide to do, the boys are going to know it's an April Fool's joke unless we're even sneakier than usual." Meaning *sneakier than we'd be if Thekla were still Empress.*

"What do you have in mind?" asked Nina.

"We should do a dummy April Fool's joke early in the day. Whether it works or not doesn't matter. They'll think we've done our best. They'll be off-guard and more susceptible to the whammy that comes next."

"I still think we should look elsewhere for our fun," said Thekla. "Our own teacher is having a crisis of the heart. Isn't it more important to help her?"

But the other Tattletales were engrossed in the notion of a double whammy. They didn't take in what Thekla was saying.

Elsewhere on the playground, the boys were shooting hoops in a loose and lazy fashion. Hector Yellow found basketball a bore, so he was drawing a picture of himself doing an ollie on a skateboard. A ways behind them, the cement mixer made its backing-up noises as a town worker positioned it to pour the new pavement by the cafeteria entrance.

"Do you think the Tattletales are going to try to pull a big April Fool's trick on us?" asked Mike Saint Michael.

"I doubt it," said Sammy Grubb. "I heard that Thekla Mustard has finally been voted out of office. Lois is the new leader of the Tattletales. Lois has more sense than Thekla."

"Thekla's not Empress anymore?" Stan Tomaski was shocked. "I wonder how she feels about *that*. She always seemed so proud of being Empress."

"A deposed ruler is a dangerous creature," said Sammy. "Not that I would mind stepping down, fellows, if someone else wanted to be Chief of the Copycats for a while."

Nobody did. Generally boys hate to have titles, to say nothing of responsibility.

Moshe Cohn shot a basket. It wobbled on the rim but then fell through. "Yessssss," said Moshe, because he wasn't very good and usually the ball wobbled off the rim in the wrong direction. He darted in and reclaimed the ball and dribbled awhile. Then he said, "Those girls sure *look* like they're plotting something."

"Girls look like they're plotting something even when they're only comparing answers to math problems," said Stan Tomaski. "It's their natural look."

"Don't you know about Miss Earth's upcoming wedding?" said Hector. "The girls overheard some proof it's really going to happen. And that's all they care about." He pointed. Miss Earth was dawdling over by the cement mixer, talking with fierce attention to Mayor Grass, who was overseeing the work. "It sure is all *she* cares about," added Hector.

Thud Tweed said, "You guys are so obsessed with girls. It's a bit weird, isn't it? If anything, shouldn't we be playing some big huge trick on Miss Earth? I mean, *she's* the power figure in the picture, isn't she?"

But one by one, the boys shook their heads. Each of them knew that Miss Earth was one of a kind. You didn't mess with Miss Earth. She was too worthy.

"Suckers," said Thud Tweed.

"You haven't even been her student for a month yet," said Sammy Grubb. "Stick around a little longer. She'll get to you. She gets to everyone. She's to teaching what Julia Child is to cooking."

"What Michelangelo is to painting," said Hector Yellow.

"What Madame Curie is to radioactivity," said Moshe Cohn.

"What Magic Johnson is to basketball," said Stan Tomaski, missing a shot.

"What Lucy Ricardo is to TV sitcoms," said Mike Saint Michael.

"What Jacques Cousteau is to the deep blue sea," said Forest Eugene Mopp.

"What Shiva is to the cycle of birth, death, and reincarnation," said Salim Bannerjee.

Thud groaned.

"Well, maybe not as much as all that," Salim said. "But she's pretty neat."

Thud rolled his eyes, indicating: You are all loony. Across the yard, Miss Earth was shrugging dramatically at something Mayor Grass was yelling over the sound of the engine. "I don't know," said Thud. "To me, she sure puts the *ham* in Hamlet."

Mrs. Cobble came out the side door and vigorously rang the hand bell. Recess was over. The kids scrambled to line up, and Miss Earth hurried away from the cement mixer.

In the commotion, Thud Tweed muttered to Lois, "Hey, Empress? Want a mole? A spy in the ointment? A secret agent at your service?"

"Call me Your Highness and call me at home," Lois muttered back. She sensed that her unformed April Fool's plan was about to hatch.

7

April Fool's:
Single Whammy

Lois Kennedy the Third had to work to open her eyes on Friday morning, April first. The evening before, she'd been strategizing on the phone till her parents had sent her to bed. She was tired.

But she saw that the day had dawned cloudless. The prospect of managing a strike against the Copycats, the Tattletales' best enemies, made the sunlight seem even cheerier. It felt good to be alive. Alive, and a little dangerous.

In houses in and around Hamlet, the Tattletales were busy equipping themselves for Stage One of their double-whammy April Fool's Day attack on the Copycats. Lois had recommended sweatshirts with pouch pockets or skirts with elastic waistbands, the better for hiding the necessary secret weapons. Six girls in six different homes exercised their trigger fingers.

And Thekla Mustard?

Thekla did not dress in her usual top-drawer finery. No power bows or neck scarves or crisp shirtwaists. For once Thekla did not care what she wore. She found an ancient Dartmouth College sweatshirt of her mom's and put that on. It hung down to her knees and made her look like a slob.

Jiggling his car keys at the bottom of the stairs, Dr. Mustard told her, "No granddaughter of Thekla Musto-welowski leaves for school looking like a slob. Go change."

Thekla's mother was washing the breakfast dishes, and the running water made enough noise to cover Thekla's reply. "I don't want to change," said Thekla.

She had so seldom talked back to her father that he didn't know whether to look at Thekla over the top of his glasses or take them off and throw them at her. He sputtered. He puffed. "My mother did not flee Poland so that her granddaughter, her namesake, could besmirch the family name by wearing apparel suitable for cleaning out the garage!"

"Grandmother Thekla cleaned rooms to make a living," said Thekla. "I'm doing this in homage to Grandmother Thekla and all her sacrifices."

Thekla wasn't really. She just wanted to feel anonymous. The line seemed to work with her dad, though, at least for the time being. He *tchchch*ed and muttered, "Well, I'll let it go this once. But don't let your mother see you."

"Mom dresses like this all the time," said Thekla.

"She doesn't go out in public," said Dr. Mustard.

Scarcely had the children settled in their seats when Miss Earth said, "I see in the *Hamlet Holler* that the Sinister Sisters' Circus is coming to town next July. It's billed as the Fourth Greatest Show on Earth, after the Academy Awards, the World Series, and *Cats*. Has anyone ever been to a circus?"

No one raised a hand.

"Perhaps we can get a school discount, even though school will be out for the summer," said Miss Earth. "I was talking about it with my fiancé yesterday."

"So you're engaged," said Thekla engagingly.

"So far as I can tell," replied Miss Earth smoothly. "We were thinking it might be nice to be married at the circus. We could be shot out of separate cannons and seal our vows with a kiss when we meet in midair. Then we could fall to the safety net, re-creating the way we fell in love. Every marriage should have a safety net, I think. What do you think?"

"But where would Father Fogarty be?" asked Fawn Petros.

"Maybe he could bless our union from the flying trapeze."

"What about your bridesmaids?" asked Carly, who was looking forward to dressing up.

"Tiptoeing across the high wire in single file?" said Miss Earth.

"Best man?" said Pearl Hotchkiss. She glanced at Sammy Grubb, who would be *her* choice for best man. Or best boy. Sammy rolled his eyes.

"Perched in the howdah of an elephant," said Miss Earth. "He could pass the rings to the elephant, and the elephant could forward them on to Father as he swung by."

"What about the maid of honor?" said Hector Yellow.

"The *matron* of honor is my mother. Grandma Earth. She can borrow some stilts from the circus tall man."

"I think it sounds great!" said Lois Kennedy the Third. "We could shower you with caramel popcorn instead of rice!"

"What day is your wedding?" asked Stan Tomaski.

Miss Earth got a wild gleam in her eye and said, "April Fool!" She laughed. "Ha ha. Gotcha gotcha."

Thekla had had enough. "Miss Earth, you're only kidding us. We know that. But what is the joke? You

55

make the whole thing sound like a—like a circus. *Are you really engaged to Mayor Grass? Will we be invited to the wedding?*"

"Never mind," said Miss Earth, looking down, with a sudden change of mood. "I oughtn't joke about serious matters."

The children felt foolish and dispirited. But after attendance was taken and the science books came out, Lois launched Stage One of the Tattletales' campaign by catching Nina's eye and giving her a little nod.

"Miss Earth," said Nina, "I was surfing the web last night and learned some serious news. Did you know that a Missing Link has been sighted in Foggy Hollow? Right here in Hamlet?"

"April Fool!" hooted the boys, and, to throw them off the scent, some of the girls did too.

"No, really," said Nina. "Look, I printed it out." She took out a document and flashed it quickly. It sure did look like an Internet printout; her brother, Pedro, had done a great job with his computer graphics program. She read from it. "'Eureka! A major scientific discovery. A mysterious creature is thought to be lurking in the woods near Hamlet, Vermont. It is six feet tall and hairy as a goon. Authorities think it could be a Missing Link, a rogue member of a species not fully simian and not yet human. It is frightening to behold, so watch out.'"

"April Fool!" "Lame one!" "Give up the game!" yelled the boys, variously.

"No, *really*," said Nina. "I knew you boys wouldn't believe me—that's why I printed it out. But I don't want to show you the picture some reporter snapped. It would be too scary."

"Boo!" "No way!" "Only thing that scares me is Thekla Mustard!"

"You would too be scared. You'd be so scared, you'd wet your pants," said Nina.

"Oh yeah?" "Says who?" "Whaddya wanna bet?"

"You think you're so brave? Have a look, then," said Nina. She marched to the front of the room and held up the little piece of paper. Challenged, all the boys but Thud lunged out of their seats to get a closer look.

"That's only a guy in a gorilla suit!" said Sammy Grubb. He turned to go back to his seat. His friends followed.

"April Fool!" shouted Lois. Then six of the girls whipped out water pistols and fired. Right at the fronts of the boys' trousers and jeans.

"Wet your pants!" screamed Lois. And the girls fell on the floor with laughter. Even Pearl Hotchkiss, who was usually above such partisanship, couldn't help guffawing. Only Thekla Mustard, her trigger finger dry and blameless, kept a stony face. Thekla wasn't ready to announce total divorce from the Tattletales yet, but she hoped her silent protest would be noticed.

The boys were frozen with shame. They sputtered and couldn't speak.

When the girls finally managed to control their screams of laughter, Thud Tweed said in a low voice, "Guess the door to the boys' room was locked." And the gales of hilarity began again.

But they wound down swiftly when Miss Earth finally managed to catch her own breath. And she had not lost it from joining in with the laughter, but from irritation.

"Sit down at once," she snapped at the boys. "Take your seats," she said to the girls, some of whom were still writhing on the floor.

The room grew still, though little flickers of nervous laughter kept burbling up here and there.

Miss Earth continued. "I have spent a good part of this school year disapproving of the power struggles that obsess the boys and the girls in this class. As you well know. But I haven't wanted to make laws and rules about how you children govern yourselves. It is part of your education to come to your own decisions about how to behave toward each other.

"However," she said, "haven't you learned anything? Today you Tattletales have *gone too far*. For the sake of civility, I must now impose martial law. While you are in my classroom, your rights to free association with your fellow Copycats or Tattletales are revoked. What you do outside the school grounds is up to you. But my commandment is law in the playgrounds, the cafeteria, the lavs, the halls, the offices, the classrooms, and the parking lot. Also the school bus," she concluded. "Do you understand me?"

No one nodded.

"Good," said Miss Earth. "Open your science books. We need to talk about the Science Fair."

The books fell open with more than a dozen sullen thumps.

"And furthermore," said Miss Earth, showing every sign of not letting the matter rest for the remainder of the day, "I'm more determined in my next decision than ever. When it comes to the Science Fair, I am going to assign you to work on your projects in pairs. Let us consider the chain of predator and prey in the natural world. Who gets chomped and who gets to do the chomping. Let's see if we can learn something about the roots of human nastiness and charity."

She was on a roll. She was a pro. She was a T-E-A-C-H-E-R, thank you very much, and a tip of the hat to the National Teachers' Association, Vermont chapter. Without even looking at her notes, she organized the Science Fair entries with flair and precision.

"Nina Bueno and Mike Saint Michael: microbes.

"Carly Garfunkel and Stan Tomaski: fleas.

"Sharday Wren and Moshe Cohn: mice.

"Anna Maria Mastrangelo and Forest Eugene Mopp: cats.

"Fawn Petros and Hector Yellow: dogs.

"Lois Kennedy the Third and Salim Bannerjee: wolves.

"Sammy Grubb—"

Miss Earth paused. Pearl Hotchkiss held her breath. She would love to be paired with Sammy Grubb. Miss Earth even suspected as much. But the appetite for revenge flared in Miss Earth's kindly breast. She gave in to the urge.

"Sammy Grubb and Thekla Mustard: bears," said Miss Earth.

Pearl Hotchkiss slumped in her chair. It was no fair.

"Thud Tweed and Pearl Hotchkiss," concluded Miss Earth, "because they're the only ones who occasionally qualify as such, may concentrate on human beings. Homo sapiens, as we're sometimes called. The knowing creatures. Though today you're acting like Homo ape-ians. At best. And that's rather insulting to the ape population."

"But—" sputtered the children, coming to life at last. "But—but—but—" they said.

"Sit on your butts!" snapped Miss Earth. And they did.

8

April Fool's:
Double Whammy

The Tattletales *had* known very well what they were doing when they decided on a Missing Link to lure the Copycats out of their seats. The Chief of the Copycats was Sammy Grubb. And the truth about Sammy Grubb was this: He wanted more than anything else to be the discoverer of a monster.

In his bedroom, a nice little room packed under the eaves at the back of his house, the old faded wallpaper was almost covered over with newspaper clippings about monsters that had been sighted—or nearly sighted—by diligent civilians armed with camcorders and digital cameras.

There were a dozen blurred photos of the Loch Ness monster in Scotland, its thumbprint of a head and long arching gooseneck caught in half-light. There were scientific diagrams of what the Abominable Snowman or Sasquatch or Bigfoot or Tippitoe, the Curse of the Andes, must look like, each based on the evidence of a single footprint found in snow or sediment. Over Sammy's desk, taking pride of place, were some awkward sketches of the five aliens from the planet Fixipuddle who had dropped in on Hamlet over the Christmas holidays.

Sammy Grubb didn't know where his obsession for the freaky and the unique came from. He didn't care, either. Sometimes at night, after piling extra blankets and some old winter coats on his bed, he'd snuggle down with a book and get warm. If there had been no recent sightings reported in the tabloids, he'd settle for a rousing story about a centaur or a griffin or a unicorn. But usually such mythical beasts were too . . . too good-natured. He preferred to fall asleep dreaming of harpies with their talons, sphinxes in their elusive wisdom, sea serpents coiling themselves around pirate galleons and dragging sailors to a watery grave.

In the morning Sammy Grubb would take a while to wake up. He'd sit in the kitchen while his mom made breakfast. He'd enjoy the faint sunshine on the scrubbed kitchen table and the fading memory of his happy dreams of monsters.

But dreams have a way of evaporating in the morning

light, and by the time he got to school, Sammy Grubb was his normal, solid, feet-on-the-ground kind of guy.

When Miss Earth released her class on the afternoon of April Fool's Day, the kids left the building with less than their usual oomph. Nobody likes to make a teacher angry. While the boys didn't feel responsible this time, they realized that they had all spent far too much time teasing the girls, goading them, tricking them and being tricked. It was the students' long habit of competition that had made Miss Earth angry. She was just fed up with the whole thing.

So Sammy wasn't all that surprised that Lois Kennedy the Third came up to him in the parking lot. "Look, I'm sorry we all got in trouble," said Lois. "Since I'm the new Empress of the Tattletales, I suppose it's my fault."

Sammy raised an eyebrow. Throughout the years that Thekla Mustard had ruled the Tattletales, had she ever apologized? Of course not. Unthinkable. With Lois in charge, maybe things would be different now.

"That's okay," he mumbled.

"I know we used that photo of the mysterious creature near Hamlet as a lure to get you boys out of your seats and up to the front of the room," said Lois. "But the story was genuine, Sammy. It showed up in the newspaper, too. Here. Take a look."

She handed over a clipping. No doubt about it: This was a newspaper photo of someone tall, hairy, and menacing. "What paper did you snip this out of?" Sammy said a bit suspiciously.

"My dad gets the *New York Times* on Tuesdays. This was in last week's Science Times section."

Lois was only partly lying. She *had* found the picture in the *New York Times,* but not in the science section. It was in Arts and Leisure, from a story about the costume designs for a new movie to be called *Curious George and King Kong: Separated at Birth?*

Sammy studied it. Though a bit well-groomed for a monster on the loose, the creature was rewardingly tall and hairy and menacing. "Foggy Hollow?" he said. "This thing has been sighted there? How come the whole town isn't talking about it?"

"I bet the grownups don't want anyone to get alarmed," said Lois. "Start a mad panic, stampede the dairy cows, that sort of thing."

"Hey, Lois!" said Carly. "Come over here! Look at this! The Foggy Hollow critter's been snooping around the Josiah Fawcett Elementary School!"

Lois and Sammy and the other kids hurried to see.

Carly was standing at the edge of the newly poured cement walk by the cafeteria door. The clean pavement was marred by a pattern of odd footprints. Though the cement was scrumbled and rucked, you could make out the basic elements of a print: a triangular stamp of a heel, three or four well-spaced toes in the front, and some sort of hook or fetlock dragging behind.

"Good sleuthing," said Lois. She had to hand it to Carly, who must have done this masterpiece the evening before, when the cement had not yet set completely. The fake footprint clinched it. Sammy Grubb was convinced.

"Okay," he said. "Might as well take a look around Foggy Hollow."

"We'll go too. If you don't mind," said Lois. "I mean, now that I'm Empress of the Tattletales, I want to set a new tone of cooperation with the Copycats."

"It's a free country. Suit yourself," said Sammy, though he'd rather have gone alone.

"All this interest in nature is unnatural. I'm not going," said Thud Tweed. "I'd rather head home and veg out in front of some R-rated videos." He trudged away with a wave. He half hoped that one of the kids would be intrigued and ask to come along. But these kids were still just kids, and Thud, one foot belligerently kicked over the threshold of adolescence, felt more alone than ever.

Anyway, it was good that no one had asked to go home with him. The R-rated videos would be later. First, a little operation to conduct . . . And Thud felt no remorse about it, given that none of the Copycats had thought of asking to go home with him.

The other kids set out. It was nearly all of them—Lois and most of the Tattletales, Sammy and the Copycats. Even Pearl Hotchkiss, who remained unaffiliated with a club, traipsed along. Only Thekla and Thud gave it a pass.

Why? wondered Lois. Well, Thekla was acting quiet and out of sorts. Maybe her eyeglass prescription needed adjustment. She looked as if she had a permanent headache these days. Lois *had* noticed Thekla's lack of participation in the Tattletale plan, Single Whammy, that morning. So Thekla wanted to do the passive resistance bit? Let her. No one would even notice.

And Thud? Lois knew why Thud wasn't coming. *Yet.*

Foggy Hollow was less a hollow than a long ribbon of wetlands that snaked around the southern edge of Hamlet, at several points running beneath the overpasses of Interstate 89. Foggy Hollow had once been the bed of a rivulet originating up near the quarries on Hardscrabble Hill, but a hundred years before, the stream had been diverted. The ravine called Foggy Hollow remembered its damp aspirations as a stream, and for much of the year the terrain of Foggy Hollow exuded a pale miasma of mist. It was a fun place to play and slop around in, though you had to watch out for gangs of high school boys experimenting with six-packs of beer and squirrel rifles.

It was a place of some mystery. Last fall, when the Siberian snow spiders had escaped their transport vehicle, they had built their terrible web in Foggy Hollow and followed the path of the gorge to the Josiah Fawcett Elementary School. Though most of the spiders had died, tatters of their durable web could still be seen.

At Lois's suggestion, the kids stopped off at Grandma Earth's Baked Goods and Auto Repair Shop to buy some doughnuts to fortify themselves. The Tattletales, Lois thought, were doing a great job of acting as they lingered over their doughnut choices. They needed at least fifteen minutes to give Thud a chance to get into the gorilla outfit they'd rented from the costume store where Carly's older sister worked over at the Ethantown Mall. So the girls elaborately fussed over whether to get Chocolate Panic or Chocolate Fever or Chocolate Hysteria doughnuts. "They're all equally nutritious," said Grandma Earth. "Hurry it up, kids. I got a distributor cap on a Ford Escort needs looking at, big-time."

Finally the children left Grandma Earth's and crossed Ethantown Road. One by one, the classmates slipped and scurried down the wet slope to the bottom of Foggy Hollow. The air seemed colder down here, and there were patches of snow and ice that the late-March sun had not been able to melt. "Keep your eyes open for more of those weird footprints," said Lois theatrically, wondering if Carly would have been clever enough to continue the ruse down here in the snow.

"So why do you think a Missing Link of any sort would choose to haunt Foggy Hollow?" asked Anna Maria Mastrangelo.

"Shhh," said Sammy Grubb. "We're not going to find it by calling 'Here, kitty kitty kitty.' Let's cut the chatter and look for signs of life."

They fell silent, if you could call slipping on the ice and muttering mild curses and crashing through bracken and tripping on tree roots being in any way silent.

Then, almost before they knew it, a creature stepped out from behind a huge rock halfway up the steep slope.

It banged its chest and roared.

Thud did such a good job that even the girls were startled. He had changed in the back room of Fawn Petros's house, which was the closest any of the Tattletales lived to Foggy Hollow. Being such a big kid, he filled out the gorilla costume impressively. In fact, in the low light of the ravine, you could hardly tell it was a gorilla outfit, which made it all the more impressive.

The kids screamed, of course, the girls as well as the boys. (The girls were just trying to make it seem authentic, they said to themselves later.) Gorilla-Thud banged his chest a couple more times and hooted like a cow that has had a songbird fly up its nose. "Only once in a lifetime," whispered Sammy Grubb with rapture, "and this is my moment—"

For a second or two, all was perfect in Sammy's world. The afternoon sun streamed into his eyes, making squinting necessary, blearing a soft light around the edges of the creature. Sammy looked and looked, as if the thing were an angel of the Lord, or Tinkerbell with gauzy wings, or some other desirable unlikeliness.

Then the creature disappeared, and the spell was broken. Though the boys tried to scramble after it, the girls did a good job of being clumsy and falling down in the way of the boys. Thud had ample time to make his getaway.

And the best part of this April Fool's joke, thought Lois, the really truly genius part of this joke, was that they could play it out for days and days. With luck, it could last the entire month of April.

9

The Dirty Double Cross

Night was beginning to roll in. Across the valley came the lowing of cows expecting to be milked. It made a nice counterpoint against the hush of cars on the interstate as commuters headed home for hot suppers. The kids regrouped by the side of Ethantown Road.

Sammy Grubb was beside himself with excitement. "I wonder what this really could be," he said. "The light was bad—so bright in our eyes—yet it clearly wasn't a bear."

"It was no laughing hyena, either," said Lois Kennedy the Third. "That critter was one big fella."

"We'd better not tell anyone about this," said Sammy.

"Why not?" Fawn Petros wasn't pretending; she had a hard time following campaigns of intrigue and deception.

72

Sammy exploded. "The good citizens of Hamlet would come out and weed-whack Foggy Hollow into a putting green! Everyone would be so curious that they'd thrash about and scare the thing to death. The media would get involved, and no good ever comes of that."

"If this is some sort of Missing Link in the chain of species," said Moshe Cohn, "let's not allow the madness of the mob to sweep him away. Remember what almost happened to E.T. in that movie? Human beings have no respect for differences among creatures." He looked so serious as he spoke, such a little egghead, that it was easy to imagine Moshe Cohn himself had come from some other planet.

"All right," said Sharday Wren. "We don't blab. We don't gab. We smack our lips together, and no *wanna-hear-a-secret*? Gotcha, Sammy."

The other kids agreed—or appeared to agree. The boys were following their leader. The girls had a secret agenda. They were going to tattle the news of the Missing Link all over town, so that when the ruse was finally revealed, the boys' shame at their own gullibility would be that much more intense. Crippling. *Delicious*.

"What happened today, dear?" asked Mrs. Mustard as Thekla came in.

"After school I spent some time shelving books for

73

Mr. Dewey at the library," said Thekla. Mrs. Mustard put down her knitting. She looked as if the notion of a little job like that sounded agreeable. But then she picked up her needles again and continued on the caps that she knitted year-round for chilly children in the mountains of Chile.

"Are things any better at school?" said Mrs. Mustard.

Thekla was about to answer, "And how could they be?" But her mother looked so hopeful that Thekla didn't have the heart to disappoint her. "Oh, Mommy," she said, "school is only school. You know that."

"But you've always loved school! And done very well too."

"I've changed. People do that, you know," she said.

Mrs. Mustard didn't comment.

"I don't care for school any longer," said Thekla. "Except for Miss Earth, of course. But she assigned me to work with Sammy Grubb on a Science Fair project. So even Miss Earth has fallen from grace."

Mrs. Mustard sighed. "No one is perfect, Thekla. You learn to love people because, mostly, they manage to be good despite their imperfections."

Thekla was about to protest this theory—there was no way that Lois Kennedy the Third, that usurper, had an ounce of human goodness in her—but then Dr. Mustard arrived home from work, and Thekla and her

74

mother both stood as he entered the room, and kissed him. Then the conversation was all about his day, as was usually the case when he came in.

Saturday was a splendid day in Hamlet, Vermont. After the fierce winter, it was revivifying to feel the sun on your skin, to see those last piles of snow heaped up at the ends of driveways shrink inch by inch, almost as you watched. Birds threw birdsong around like nobody's business. Snowdrops and a few daffodils showed up on the sunniest slopes.

But few people in Vermont noticed the bright day. Instead, the town was abuzz with gossip about the Missing Link.

"Don't say I told you," said Anna Maria Mastrangelo to Widow Wendell on the front porch of Clumpett's General Store, "but there's a tall and hairy creature lurking about Foggy Hollow these days."

"I wonder if he's married," said Widow Wendell.

Inside the store, Bucky and Olympia Clumpett, the owners, were listening with bemused expressions as Nina Bueno spoke to them. "If I were you, I'd double-bolt my back door at night. There's no telling what kind of appetite a monster like that has, and you might see some serious damage done to your stock of potato chips, corn chips, wheat chips, and a whole range of dips."

Over at the tap-dance class in the Flora Tyburn Memorial Gym, Sharday Wren was performing an interpretive *pas de deux* with an imaginary monster. She was effective and stylish, but her teacher, Hank McManus, said, "Sharday, we're supposed to be working on our triple-shuffle-and-repeats."

At Grandma Earth's Baked Goods and Auto Repair Shop, Fawn Petros was trying to explain the monster to Grandma Earth and Miss Earth. Miss Earth, helping her mother out behind the counter, was tossing jelly doughnuts into sacks, and when Fawn finally managed to mention, "Oh, by the way, we saw a monster in Foggy Hollow yesterday," it was only in a whisper and nobody heard her. Miss Earth was too busy murmuring something private to her mother. Fawn wondered if Thekla was right, and there was trouble in Loveland.

At the library, Thekla Mustard was looking up pictures of Huge Hairy Beasts in the encyclopedia. "What do you think of these lunks?" she asked Mr. Dewey indignantly. "Real, or in-your-dreams?"

"Not in *my* dreams," said Mr. Dewey. "Not real, either. Listen, your common Newfoundland moose is scarier than these figments of imagination."

Mayor Grass came into the library. "I'm looking for the phone number of the Upper Valley Barbershop Quartet," he said to Mr. Dewey. "Need your help in the research department. Trying to get my hands on a tenor."

"Maybe I could help," said Thekla boldly. "I can thumb through a phone book as well as Mr. Dewey can."

"Give it a rest, Thekla," said Mayor Grass a bit wearily. "Do me a favor. Enjoy being a kid before grown-up concerns wear you down."

Mayor Grass in a grumpy mood? How unlike him, thought Thekla. Maybe he's upset about what Miss Earth said to him in the meadow the other day. Thekla went swanning about the room, sniffing for clues of love gone wrong. Mayor Grass waved her away, though, and she had no option but to go. Darn.

Lois Kennedy the Third's family stopped by the Mango Tree to pick up some chicken korma. Salim Bannerjee's dad ran the Mango Tree, the only Indian restaurant in Winsor County. Salim was helping his dad by folding the little takeout boxes. Lois took the opportunity to say loudly, "I just couldn't sleep a wink all night, Salim, remembering that monster in Foggy Hollow!"

"Shhh!" said Salim, which made everybody listen all the harder when Lois went on, "Oh, sorry. I forgot we weren't supposed to tell anyone we saw a monstrous beast in the woods yesterday. Lips sealed. Mum's the word. I just *love* chicken korma, don't you, Salim?"

And so it went, all day Saturday. By Sunday morning, the congregations at Saint Mary in the Tombstones and the Hamlet Congregational/Unitarian Church were all buzzing during their respective coffee hours. The adults looked amused and slightly weary, but they listened. The news was out. When Lois, walking home Sunday noontime, heard Flossie Fingerpie screaming the latest gossip to deaf Old Man Fingerpie, she knew her campaign to embarrass Sammy Grubb was working even better than she had anticipated.

She was a much better Empress of the Tattletales than Thekla dried-out-Mustard!

Thud Tweed spent Sunday afternoon lying on the sofa with the channel changer and a liter bottle of Dr Pepper. The rubberized mask of a gorilla head was propped on a side table. His mother, a famous country-western singer known as Petunia Whiner when she left the privacy of her home, passed through with a fax.

"Darling Thaddeus," she said, using Thud's given name, "feet on the sofa is one thing, but must you insist on decapitating jungle animals and displaying their craniums on my valuable antiques? I found that *demi-lune* at a Sotheby's auction, and it was very dear."

"It's fake," said Thud, pointing to the gorilla mask.

"Oh, that's all very well, then," she said crisply. (When she wasn't singing, Mildred Tweed spoke in a Mayfair accent, since she was from London.) "Are you in for dinner? I'm planning lamb chops and baby peas. I'm going to cook them myself."

Thud knew that his mother hated to cook. She had employed a personal chef ever since her first platinum single, "Overate, Overweight, Over You." "What, has Maria Consuelo gone to Caracas again?" he asked.

"Yes," said Mrs. Tweed. She perched herself on the edge of a delicate chair upholstered in yellow and silver striped silk. "I am afraid I have some bad news, Thud." She looked at the fax as if for inspiration, or to be reminded what the bad news was.

Thud got a metallic taste in his mouth, like tarnish from an old fork. He sat up. "Dad? Everything all right in prison?"

"Your father is fine. He expects to get out on good behavior in a matter of months. No, it's more mundane than that. My manager called this morning and faxed me this afternoon. It seems that Madonna has had to cancel her Candy Striper Tour due to swollen adenoids. My manager has convinced the booking agency to offer an appearance by Petunia Whiner instead. Now, you know sales of the new album haven't been brisk, but Petunia's fans are feeling her pain, I mean with your dad

79

in jail and all. So the long and the short of it is that Petunia Whiner needs to go on tour."

"When?"

"Almost instantly. Now, darling, don't pout; it's not for long. A few weeks at most. Some really lovely places. We're talking Tulsa, Des Moines, Duluth, maybe Schenectady, and then when we're tight and rockin', we'll hit Boston, Atlanta, Philly, Denver. Maybe Seattle, and listen, honey, definitely we'll do a big finish in Manhattan. You want to come with me?"

Thud flopped back on the sofa. He picked up the gorilla head. He spoke to his mother but stared the gorilla in the rubberized eyes as if addressing it.

"You walk out now, it'll be 'Overate, Overweight, Over You.' The live version."

"Thaddeus. Please. I don't like this any more than you—"

He took pity—a little, anyway. "Mom, let's review the facts, okay? A: Hamlet, Vermont, hardly knows the twentieth century has already come and gone. The kids in school are nice enough, but they're backward, inno-cent, and dumb. B: I don't really like it here. But I can stand it here. C: I definitely don't want to spend three or four weeks in hotels with a private tutor who hates my guts."

"I don't want you to decide all at once," said Mrs.

Tweed. "And Thaddeus—I'm sorry. I was hoping not to have to do this."

"Mumsy Mumsworthy," said Thud, "what you want and what Petunia Whiner wants are two different things. Don't think I don't get it." He slipped the gorilla mask on. Peering through the nostril holes, he turned his attention back to the TV. "And don't worry about my getting into trouble."

"I'd rather you came with me," said Mrs. Tweed softly.

"Grrrrrrrrrrrrrr," said the gorilla. But when Mrs. Tweed left to begin torturing some lamb chops, Thud let his eyes close behind the gorilla mask.

Sometimes it was easier to be someone else. When his mother was stay-at-home Mildred Tweed, she seemed like a glass of skim milk. But she became peppy as ginger beer when she was dolled up as Petunia Whiner. He could see why she had taken to performing as Petunia Whiner, Nashville diva. A little play-acting was helpful. It gave her a different view on life.

But in his heart of hearts, Thud supposed he was more Thud than Thaddeus. He had made so many mistakes in his life—just like his father had done!—and he didn't want to make more. Maybe the trick was just to stay behind a mask, like this rubberized face he had on.

It rucked up against the back of his neck and chafed,

but he didn't take it off. In the morning he was supposed to return the mask and outfit to Carly Garfunkel, whose sister Paula worked in the costume store over at the Ethantown Mall. Paula had rented it for the April Fool's Day joke but was intending to return it Monday morning when the shop opened.

What if Thud were to continue the joke? What if he were to deliver the costume to Carly, do high-fives with the Tattletales, and then pull a dirty double cross on them? He could let Sammy in on the ruse, and the girls might think there really *was* a Missing Link on the loose. They could snooker the girls somehow.

Sure, Sammy had said no April Fool's Day joke on the girls. But he might have a different opinion once the boys were rudely shamed in public. And what could be trickier than to do an April Fool's joke after the fact?

He'd tell Carly in the morning that he would return the costume to the store himself. He hoped Paula Garfunkel wouldn't be at the register when he got there, but in any event, Paula didn't know who he was by sight.

Thud was trying to fit in. Fit in with the girls, fit in with the boys. He was too big to fit in, and he didn't have much practice having real friends. But he was trying.

"Mom," he bellowed, "can you at least take me over to the Ethantown Mall tomorrow after school before you leave on your tour?"

"Why, I'd be delighted, darling," called his mom. He could tell she thought she was making things all right.

"Either I will or Harold will," she amended, speaking of the butler/chauffeur. "There's so much to do to get ready. I may not have the time."

Before he went to bed, Thud switched on the computer and printed out a little note for the next day.

> *Hey, want to know who's on your side? Meet me in Foggy Hollow an hour after school gets out, and I'll let you in on a secret.*

10

Sabotage to Boot

On Monday morning, Miss Earth was more or less back to normal. Her manner was brisk but not unkind. Still, she shook her head when Lois Kennedy the Third asked her to rethink the boy-girl pairings for the Science Fair assignments. Lois said, "Many studies have shown that girls work better with girls than with boys. Don't you want us to do our best and succeed in the Science Fair?"

"It's like fractions and decimals," offered Fawn helpfully. "Fractions like fractions, and decimals, decimals. They don't want to convert all the time."

"Whether you consider yourself a fraction or a decimal, I want all of you always to do your best in whatever cruel situation you find yourselves," said Miss Earth.

"I've thrown you into the deep end this time, kids; you have to learn to swim sooner or later. There are few adults who don't have to deal with the opposite sex every day of their lives. As folks say these days: Get used to it."

She might have gone on to say more, as her face had that *And let me add another thing while we're on the subject* look to it. But Mayor Timothy Grass stopped by, brandishing a bouquet of pussy willows he had picked at the town dump. Miss Earth became distracted. Thekla, watching closely, wondered if these springtime buds constituted a peace offering. Was Miss Earth rushing around trying to find a vase because she was charmed, or because she didn't want to stand there and have to look Mayor Grass in the eye and say, *It's not working, Tim— I'm going to have to leave?* It was so hard to tell.

Thud Tweed had decided that if Lois and the other Tattletales saw him hobnobbing with Sammy Grubb on the playground, they might guess a double cross was about to happen. The note he'd printed out last night would do the trick.

Thud wrapped the note around a strip of bubble gum. When lunchtime came and the kids began to file out for recess, Thud dropped the message on Sammy's desk. Sammy would find it when recess was over.

What Thud didn't know was that Thekla Mustard was still exercising her canny eyes. She saw him leave Sammy a note.

Thekla was happy about very little these days. She had been deposed as Empress! Forced to live life as a common citizen without exceptional status! And also she'd been paired with Sammy Grubb in the Science Fair project on bears. *Bears.* Really, how low could you go?

After the kids had gone outdoors, Thekla snuck back in under pretext of having to use the girls' lavatory. She found the note Thud had left for Sammy. She opened it, carefully flattened it, and read it.

Hey, want to know who's on your side? Meet me in Foggy Hollow an hour after school gets out, and I'll let you in on a secret.

Aha! After his collaboration with the Tattletales, was Thud planning on double-crossing them?

Though Thekla had little respect for Lois as Empress, she still hadn't formally resigned from the club she had started herself. And she didn't want to stand by and see the Tattletales lose face. So Thekla decided to nip Thud's little exercise in the bud. Just in case it was a double cross.

The former Empress of the Tattletales took another piece of paper and wrote a note on it.

There are traitors at every turn.
signed,
a well-wisher

Then she wrapped her note around the gum and left it where Sammy would find it.

Thekla hoped that by alerting Sammy Grubb to the presence of a traitor—Thud Tweed—she could perform a little sabotage against the reign of Lois Kennedy the Third, the current and, she hoped, short-lived Empress of the Tattletales.

Thekla might have written her message out more directly, but years of being Empress of the Tattletales had taught her the virtues of being mysterious. She preferred a cloak-and-dagger tone. If she got impatient, she could always just call Sammy Grubb on the phone and rat on Thud Tweed. What was to stop her? But she'd save that for a later tactic, if needed. It felt good to be working solo, for once.

Pleased with herself, she tossed Thud's original note toward the trash basket and ran out of the room.

Jasper Stripe, the janitor, was just coming in the door

from outside. A gust of spring air blew Thud's note to Sammy Grubb onto the floor. Jasper Stripe picked it up and put it on Miss Earth's desk. Then he emptied the trash basket of its treasure lode of apple cores and milk cartons.

When Miss Earth came back into her classroom a few minutes before recess was over, she took off her yellow-grosbeak shawl and hung it on the back of her chair. Then she saw the flattened piece of paper on her desk and read its message.

> *Hey, want to know who's on your side? Meet me in Foggy Hollow an hour after school gets out, and I'll let you in on a secret.*

And then—mercy on her soul—Miss Earth made a serious mistake.

Miss Earth decided this was a little note from Timothy Grass. He must have dropped it on her desk when he came in with the pussy willows. He wanted to meet her in the spring woods an hour after she got off from work. Often they met at the Blue Willow Café, but perhaps he wanted to walk in the woods with her. They'd had a little disagreement recently. . . .

She'd never known Tim to type a note before. It made the invitation seem a little formal. She wondered if everything was all right.

She could really use a nice bit of exercise, what with all this tiresome nonsense from her students.

She put the typed note into the front of her lesson plan book so she could look at it. All through the afternoon, she was so distracted with the notion of her rendezvous with Tim that she didn't pick up on the early-warning signs of trickery in the works.

Sammy Grubb, meanwhile, read the note Thekla Mustard had left for him. *Traitors at every turn?* He didn't get it. He shrugged noncommittally and popped the gum into his mouth, where it stayed for about twelve seconds until Miss Earth reminded him there was no gum chewing in school. Then he wrapped up the gum in the first scrap of paper that came to hand—Thekla's note—and deposited it in the trash basket. Sammy didn't really think that the world was full of traitors.

When school let out, Thud didn't join the other kids on the school bus. Harold was waiting with the town car as directed. The gorilla head sat in the backseat, where Thud had stored it. He intended to show it to Sammy as proof that he, Thud, had been the Missing Link.

Thud told Harold to drive to the public library. There was easy access to Foggy Hollow from the slope beyond the graveled parking area. While Thud kept his appointment with Sammy Grubb, he could have Harold go in and do some research on Homo sapiens, Thud and Pearl's Science Fair project.

An hour after school let out, Sammy Grubb was nowhere near Foggy Hollow. He'd never received Thud's note, after all.

Sammy would have *liked* to be there, trying to catch another glimpse of the Missing Link, but his parents were in a bit of a financial pinch. His mom had been let go from her job at Valley Electronics, and Sammy was pitching in by helping his dad do some grounds work at a McMansion over in Woodstock. There was raking of leaves and restacking of firewood, that sort of thing. His dad got paid ten bucks an hour, and Sammy got five, of which he gave three to his parents and kept two for himself. So, on the floodlit lawns, he worked till well after dark and earned some decent cash.

At the same time, Thekla Mustard was stomping into her house. Her mother looked up. "No friends to meet today?" said Mrs. Mustard. Thekla didn't even bother to answer. She crashed upstairs and pulled out her desk chair and sat down to begin the Science Fair project. BEARS, she wrote on the top of the page. BEARS BEARS BEARS. WHO CARES CARES CARES? She realized that a bear looked something like a Missing

Link. She wondered if Thud Tweed was loitering in Foggy Hollow waiting for Sammy, who wouldn't show up since he hadn't gotten Thud's message. Ha ha.

But Thekla took little satisfaction from her trick. She was finding that being a solo agent wasn't very rewarding. Had she quit the Tattletales? What if she *had* quit, and nobody even noticed? Herself included?

Salim Bannerjee walked home that afternoon. He considered his first curious year in the United States. The various visitors to Hamlet, Vermont. Siberian snow spiders at Halloween. Baby Tusker, an elephant ghost, at Thanksgiving. Aliens from Fixipuddle over the Christmas break! And then, just when spring showed up, mutant chickens with fiery opinions. Hamlet was a small town, but it sure had its share of celebrity visitors over the holidays. And that wasn't even counting Meg Snoople, top investigative reporter.

But those who come to visit very rarely stay. Most of the spiders had met untimely ends. The ghost of Baby Tusker had been adopted by other ghosts. The aliens had flown away. And Seymour the Flameburper was still dead, and nothing would bring him back.

What was to keep those you loved solid on the ground, steady through time? Salim knew through experience, as well as from his Hindu father's observations, that all things change in time.

This thought gave Salim some comfort, though he knew that dead creatures couldn't change back into live ones.

Meanwhile, Lois Kennedy the Third was walking her dog, Reebok, along Squished Toad Road near Old Man Fingerpie's farm. She considered stopping in to see Beatrice the Flameburper.

Old Man Fingerpie's house looked dark. Lois didn't like to trespass. But she did anyway. She pushed open the barn door.

Doozy Dorking—always easily startled—exploded in a combustion of fright and launched herself to a rail. She could manage an altitude of about five feet for a period of about two seconds—just long enough to get to a roost off the ground if there happened to be a convenient perch nearby. She clucked furiously at Lois.

Beatrice, however, paid no attention. She was distracted. The little Flameburper—well, not quite so little anymore—was jabbing bits of straw together. They kept falling apart. Beatrice looked as if she were trying to knit without any knitting needles. She seemed frustrated.

"Hi, honey, I'm home," singsonged Lois softly.

It was Beatrice's turn to start. A little blat of flame jetted from her mouth. Reebok took one look and bolted. Doozy clucked and flung herself against a wall, knocking herself out. Lois said, "Jeepers, sorry! Don't get excited! What's bugging you, baby?"

The little clutch of fibrous craft straw was burned into a few charred bits. Beatrice threw back her head in frustration and alarm and, to the extent she could, wailed.

"All right, I'm leaving," said Lois. "I never meant to scare you so badly, BeaBea baby. You're so jumpy these days." She backed out and went to look for Reebok.

Miss Earth pulled her motorcycle into the small lot behind the Hamlet Free Community Library. She parked next to a flashy limo—Thud Tweed's family, no doubt.

She raised her hand to wave through the window at Mr. Dewey, but his head was bent over a pile of books. So Miss Earth pulled her bird-covered shawl about her and wandered into the woods behind the library. The ground sloped down gently for a while, and for the first minute or two she could see the backs of Clumpett's General Store, the library, and the Hamlet House of Beauty. But nobody saw her.

During the following week, many people stopped to consider that at the very moment Miss Earth walked away from her motorcycle, under coercion or of her own volition, they had been within the sound of her voice. Some had been shopping at Clumpett's. Some had been browsing in the library. Some had been having their hair done at the Hamlet House of Beauty. They kicked themselves for following their own concerns instead of staring out the windows to make sure that their fellow citizens remained safe and well.

But no one saw Miss Earth leave the muddy parking area and disappear into the woods. No one admired her well-combed hair or her freshened lipstick. No one was there to wave goodbye, or bid her *beware*.

Quite a while later, Thud Tweed climbed out of the ravine. He'd waited on a rock until he got chilly, then he'd wandered irritably back and forth. But Sammy Grubb had never shown up. What a waste of time.

Harold had downloaded and printed out some articles on Homo sapiens. Now he was sitting in the front seat, listening to the news on Vermont Country Radio. "Funny, they don't say anything about a Missing Link being sighted in the Upper Valley region of Vermont," said Harold conversationally as Thud climbed into the back of the car.

"Home," snapped Thud.

He could call Sammy, of course. Maybe that was a

better idea. But not tonight. He was sick of everyone at the moment.

Thud was in such a funk that, as the car accelerated, he threw the gorilla mask out the car window. The thing rolled down into a gully, filled with water, and sank. Good riddance.

11

Foul Play?

The first inkling of trouble came when the school bell sounded. The children of the Josiah Fawcett Elementary School usually milled around in playground games and conversations, but when the morning bell rang, the custom was to line up by class in front of your teacher. Ms. Frazzle corralled the kindergartners. Mrs. Messett, Mr. Pilsky, Ms. Amberly, Mrs. Farmersdottir all collected their students.

No one stood in Miss Earth's spot.

This had never happened before. The schoolyard fell silent. Out of habit, Miss Earth's students lined up anyway, but it seemed peculiar.

"Miss Earth's motorcycle is not in the parking lot," said Jasper Stripe. "Maybe she had a flat on the way to school. Well, I'll take you lot in."

Soberly, the kids filed into the school behind the janitor.

"Uhhh," he said when they had all taken their seats, "I'm not sure what we do next."

Thekla Mustard raised her hand.

"What's wrong, you got a cramp in your arm?" asked Jasper Stripe.

"I'm trying to attract your attention so I can speak," she said.

"I never met a female who needed someone's attention in order to speak," said the janitor. "Usually they just blab whether anyone is listening or not."

Thekla opened her mouth to blab a protest at this tomfool biased notion. But she decided it was better to stay focused. "I'm trying to tell you how the classroom works. First you take attendance. Then we say the Pledge of Allegiance. Then we get five minutes to water the plants and feed the frog and the gerbils. Then—"

"Whoa, one step at a time. I'll never keep this straight. Okay, attendance. Everybody who's here is here, right? Good. Now the Pledge. I pledge a wedgie in the pants of the United Chefs of America. . . .

"What?" he said when no one laughed. "What?"

"Mr. Stripe," said Thekla coldly, "we don't make *fun* of the *Pledge of Allegiance*."

"I was only trying to cheer you up," he said. "So you

97

wouldn't be nervous or anything. About your teacher's being missing."

That was when the children began to get nervous.

Jasper Stripe lasted only a few more minutes. When Principal Hetty Buttle showed up to take over, the janitor fled gratefully.

"Children," said Principal Buttle, "Miss Earth has been detained for a while. I'll sit in. What does her lesson plan remark for today?" She flipped the book open. She didn't notice the note inside the front cover. She just saw *9 a.m.: Pair up to work on Science Fair projects.*

"Let's pair up to work on Science Fair projects," said Principal Buttle decisively.

No one moved. "Go on. Pair. Have you partners? Good. Move your chairs so you can work with your partners."

Reluctantly the kids scraped their chairs out of the usual order. Principal Buttle was surprised to see that the pairings were all boy-girl. "Some progress happening in this room!" she observed. "Now, children—to work." She sat down at the desk to leaf through a catalog devoted to selling goods of interest to school principals: staffs and rods for the beating of children, inspirational posters featuring cats clinging to the end of a knotted rope, that sort of thing.

Principal Buttle's mind wandered. She wished she could redecorate the principal's office in a science fiction theme. She imagined a principal's chair with a headrest and a button console and a built-in TV monitor and a seat belt in case of earthquake or attack by comet. She couldn't find a single item to fill her needs, though.

The children muttered instead of working on their projects.

"I don't think Miss Earth has ever been late for school," said Hector Yellow to Fawn Petros.

"I didn't think she'd know *how* to be late," confessed Fawn.

Lois Kennedy the Third said to Salim Bannerjee, "We're supposed to be working on wolves. I wonder if there is a wolf on the prowl locally. Could Miss Earth have been eaten by a wolf?"

"Anything's possible," said Salim.

Thekla Mustard was too cross to talk to Sammy Grubb. But she talked to herself within his earshot. "First I get booted out of the position of Empress. And now this. Really, I don't know what the world is thinking of."

"The world doesn't consider your needs particularly, does it?" said Sammy Grubb. A longtime adversary of Thekla's, secretly he felt a little sorry for her these days. But of course, he didn't want it to show.

"What's that buzzing sound? Have the first black flies of the season hatched? Oh, it's a Sammy Grubb talking. What's it saying, I wonder?" Thekla peered meanly into his face.

Pearl Hotchkiss was happy to be paired with Thud Tweed for one reason and one reason alone: If they were sitting facing each other, then Thud couldn't sneak up behind her and pull her braid. "What do you think happened to Miss Earth?" she whispered.

"Mental health day. She's gone to Hanover to have a pedicure, see a matinee, buy some new spark plugs for her Kawasaki 8000 Silver Eagle. How should I know? People flit out of your life all the time. Without a moment's notice. Who cares?"

Pearl said to herself, He's thinking of his dad. And maybe she was right. But Thud was also thinking of his mom, about to go on tour again, when she'd promised. She'd *promised*.

By noon Principal Buttle had about had it with substitute teaching. She directed Ms. Frazzle to take the afternoon kindergarten class into Miss Earth's room. "Do something fun!" she ordered them.

"What?" said Ms. Frazzle dourly. "Make a scale model of the Brooklyn Bridge with toothpicks? Translate an episode of *Arthur* into Late Sanskrit? Compute to the tenth decimal place the number of gallons of mucus I have wiped from these kindergarten noses since flu season began? I'll tell you, this batch of kids is way ahead of itself."

"We wanna play stock market!" her kids chorused. "Nikkei, Nasdaq, Standard and Poor. Watch the Dow go through the floor!"

"Silence!" roared Ms. Frazzle, and sat down to read aloud from the *Wall Street Journal* about emerging Asian markets. The kindergartners listened raptly.

"Uh, Ms. Frazzle?" said Moshe Cohn. "May I interrupt? Have you heard anything more about Ms. Earth?"

"I never repeat the depressing things I hear," said Ms. Frazzle, which wasn't encouraging.

When school let out, for once the kids didn't round themselves up into little knots of friends and allies. The day felt too odd—unfinished. Those kids who walked home walked—by themselves. Those kids who usually took the bus took the bus, but the chatter was subdued. The bus driver, Mrs. Brill, was so unused to silent passengers that she kept shaking her head to check her hearing.

At various supper tables around town, it was clear that the news of Miss Earth's disappearance had gotten out. Clear, that is, because every parent, to the last one of them, shrugged his or her shoulders and made a joke and changed the subject. A sure sign that something was seriously wrong.

In the morning, there was no more disguising the obvious. When the school bus rattled past Grandma Earth's Baked Goods and Auto Repair Shop, every child sitting on the right-hand side of the bus could see that the bakery was not doing its usual brisk business of doughnuts and coffee. The front windows were dark. Taped to the door was a sign featuring one word in a scrawl: CLOSED.

The playground was eerily quiet. People whispered the news that Miss Earth's motorcycle had been discovered parked behind the library.

Foul play could not be ruled out.

12

The Adolescence
of a Flameburper

For the children in Miss Earth's class, the next day began miserably and continued worse.

First they realized that their substitute teacher was to be the school nurse, Pinky Crisp. They liked her well enough, but she was driven by enthusiasms mostly having to do with personal hygiene. All she wanted to do was discuss the chemical composition of personal effluvia like earwax, split ends, toenails, and dandruff. When she neared the subject of common body odors— their varieties, causes, and remedies—Hector Yellow raised his hand.

"Nurse Crisp?" he said. "I have a delicate constitution. I'm afraid if we follow this line of discussion much further, I may lose my breakfast."

"A wonderful opportunity to discuss the vomit

reflex!" said Nurse Crisp brightly, but when Hector began to go an asparagus color, she suggested that they draw diagrams of the digestive system instead.

The day deteriorated. Clouds moved in stealthily, and before long it was raining. "Who could conduct a search of Hamlet in this downpour?" asked Thekla Mustard at lunch. "It's raining cats and dogs."

Recess was indoors due to the deluge. The Copycats and Tattletales, with both Pearl Hotchkiss and Thud Tweed in attendance, took over a corner of the cafeteria and discussed the situation. But no one had any inkling about where their teacher might have gone.

"Perhaps," said Thekla Mustard pointedly, "she fell in love with someone other than Mayor Grass and eloped."

"Who else *is* there?" asked Moshe Cohn.

"Oh, a certain tenor she might have found attractive," said Thekla.

"There are lots of people in other places who have a fair amount of zip and charm," said Carly Garfunkel. "Remember we thought she might fall in love with that newscaster, Chad Hunkley? Maybe it's happened."

"She doesn't even like TV. She wouldn't go for no newscaster," protested Sharday Wren. "No way, girl."

"Mayor Grass might know something," said Thekla. "I heard him say, 'I'll always remember you like this.'

Did he *know* she was going to disappear?"

"If he knew," said Carly, "he'd be responsible. What are you suggesting, Thekla?"

"I'm just asking questions!" said Thekla.

"Are you accusing Mayor Grass of committing . . . a crime?"

"Nobody is accusing anyone of anything," snapped Thekla Mustard.

But the words had been said. The thought had been voiced.

For the afternoon lessons, Nurse Crisp decided to deliver an impromptu lecture called "The Mystery of Human Emotions: Endocrinology Today." While Nurse Crisp rattled on about the secrets of the pituitary gland, Lois wrote a note.

ATTENTION,
ALL OF MISS EARTH'S STUDENTS

The time for petty partisan bickering is over (for now). Miss Earth is missing. We must band together and care for each other, with or without the help of endocrine, which according to Loudmouth Crisp up there Can Be Our Friend. Why not come to the Fingerpies' barn today after school, and we can look in on Beatrice the

Flameburper? This invitation is open to ALL, not just the bold Tattletales and the cringing, feckless Copycats. You too, Thud and Pearl.

signed,
Empress Lois

She sent the piece of paper to make its way around the room, and one by one the kids nodded. Everyone signed on, except for Pearl, who had to babysit her six younger brothers and sisters after school and who never got to do anything fun.

Despite the continuing rain, the children felt a little cheerier to have something to do. They walked in single file up Squished Toad Road, taking care not to get hit by any cars coming over the hill from Puster Center. When they got to the barn, Flossie Fingerpie was busy fitting a length of new pipe to a water line. She was up to her ears in cow slop and valve grease. "Boy, am I going to miss it when good old Vermont barn muck gives way to imported designer manure," she said.

"We came to see Beatrice," said Lois.

"Be my guest. Be her guest, I mean. I think she's feeling a little antsy. Do her good to have some company. I've penned her in over there in the whelping stall till she learns some manners."

Most of the kids were accustomed to the richness of barn smells. But Thud, for whom the sharp odor of urine in New York City subway stairwells was more familiar, said, "Yuck, who pooped in here?"

"Just about everybody," answered Flossie. "Except for toilet-trained humans, of course."

Since the children had last been to visit, the whelping stall had been lined with sheets of tin. "What's all this about?" called Lois.

"Beatrice has been going through a stage," said Flossie. "Maybe she's a teenager already, at least counting in chicken years. She's rude, she's sassy, she keeps setting the straw on fire. She seems tense and irritable. Every now and then, right out of the blue, she has a little conniption fit. I think it's just her version of foul language—hah, *fowl* language! Get it? I'm such a card, I should be a writer for that Simpsons show. Oh, shoot." The pipe she was working on clattered to the ground and hit her work boot. "So I redecorated her winter home in fireproof tin. I'm piping over a water line just in case her adolescent moods get the better of her. Don't want to lose the barn the way we almost lost the general store a few weeks ago."

"She's not an adolescent yet!" said Lois. "She just hatched a month ago."

"She won't eat, she puts on airs, she makes fun of her

mother, she'd go out and not say where she'd been when she got back, if I let her go out," said Flossie. "Chicks grow up fast, and remember, this little chickadee is genetically altered. I read in the *Farmer's Almanac* that cloned critters suffer the complaints of old age earlier than their natural-born cousins. Maybe the same is true of genetically tickled critters. She sure looks like an adolescent to me. What d'you lot make of it?"

They crowded around the whelping pen. Doozy Dorking was trying to think her own thoughts, and she had climbed onto an overturned plastic milk crate. Beatrice, who did seem to be enjoying a growth spurt, was stalking around at the base of it. Every now and then she'd throw her little head back and cackle. She made a dryish sound, like an old-fashioned windup toy that shot out sparks when its key was turned. Beatrice's sparks were shaped like tiny spears, and at the heart of each was a real flame. Luckily, so far, the flames were burning themselves out before the sparks landed on anything flammable.

Then Beatrice lifted her little wings, and out came the little arms. They were a sort of brownish green, the color of goose droppings. At the ends of the little arms unfolded little claws, two fingers and a kind of backward-jointed thumb. The claws took hold of the latticed side of the milk crate and shook it.

"Squawk!" fussed Doozy Dorking.

"*Hisss-kkkk,*" answered Beatrice.

The kids did not say, "Awwww." They did not say, "How adorable!"

"She's Nature's Big Boo-Boo," said Thud. "She's Frankenstein's Chicken."

When Beatrice couldn't dislodge her stepmother, she threw herself down in the dirt and began to thump herself up and down, as if she were doing belly flops on a trampoline, only the dirt didn't flop back.

"That's just like my teenage sister Paula," said Carly. "When her boyfriend doesn't call, she smashes herself on the bed over and over and cries."

"I'd rather be a genetically altered chicken with an abbreviated life span than a teenager," said Hector Yellow. The others could not help but agree.

"But we *will* be teenagers soon," Salim reminded them. "All things change, including us."

Beatrice kicked her little horned feet into the soil and whined. Doozy Dorking rolled her eyes.

Then Beatrice picked herself up and kicked her way sullenly across the whelping pen to a corner behind a plastic bucket. There she burrowed into a little cave of molted feathers, straw, and random barn refuse that she seemed to have knitted together into a nest. Apparently she had learned how to do basketweaving. She squatted inside and began to work at the construction with her little hands. Every now and then, a scary little blat of sparks, like miniature fireworks, came out the door. She seemed to know enough not to set her own house on fire, anyway.

"What's she doing?" asked Forest Eugene Mopp.

"I think she's building herself a little sleeping bag. Or a feathery igloo," said Nina Bueno.

"She's pretty good at it," said Forest Eugene. And she was. After glaring at them for a while, Beatrice fitted into place a round door, something like a furry manhole cover, and retreated into her own private space.

Doozy Dorking hopped down and immediately went and drank some water to calm her nerves. The kids threw some seed corn to pep her up. But Beatrice must have heard them, because she kicked open the round door and ran out, and using both beak and hands, she collected all the seed corn before Doozy could figure out what was happening.

Then she retired into her furry cell and pulled her door closed again.

"She's a greedy little thing," said Lois admiringly.

"She's a teenager. She's got a healthy appetite. She's growing by leaps and bounds," said Sammy.

In the various homes in Hamlet that night, rumors ran rampant about Miss Earth's odd disappearance. None of the parents wanted to alarm their children, but in a town as small as Hamlet, very little happens that isn't talked about.

In Sammy Grubb's house, his mom heated up some frozen fish sticks. When the family gathered in the kitchen, Mr. Grubb turned up the radio to catch the news. But Miss Earth's disappearance wasn't mentioned.

"She left her motorbike behind the library," said Mrs. Grubb. "Wonder why."

"Or somebody else left it there," said Mr. Grubb. "Someone trying to throw the cops off the trail."

"What trail?" asked Sammy, whose mind had been wandering along the trail of the Missing Link. He was wondering if there was any connection between the appearance of a Missing Link and the disappearance of Miss Earth. But he couldn't imagine who would know.

At the Mango Tree, Salim Bannerjee packed some vegetables and rice into a pint container and handed it to Mayor Grass. Salim was too embarrassed to ask Mayor Grass how he was doing during this time of crisis—his sweetheart missing and all that. So Salim only said, "That'll be four dollars and sixty-five cents."

Mayor Grass's hand was bandaged, and he struggled to get the change out of his pocket. "Sorry, I'm clumsy today," he said. "Can't even cook for myself, so I'm grateful for the Mango Tree."

"How'd you hurt your hand?" asked Salim.

"Cut it on the cement mixer the other evening," said Mayor Grass. "Silly me." He dropped a quarter in the tip jar.

"Hey, thanks," said Salim, and watched Timothy Grass leave, favoring his right hand as he used his shoulder to push open the door.

At Lois Kennedy the Third's house, as Mrs. Kennedy ladled a lentil cassoulet into handmade blue bowls, she said, "Lois, what's being said in the classroom about your teacher's absence?"

"Yuck, I hate lentils," said Lois, stalling for time.

"Yuck," said her younger brothers. "Yuck, yuck."

"Lois," said her mother, "how many times have I told you, monkey see, monkey do?"

When her mother had returned the tureen to the oven to keep warm, Lois leaned over to her younger brothers and said, "Monkey pee, monkey doo-doo."

This riled up her siblings into such unquestioned heights of hilarity that they didn't calm down for half an hour, by which time Mrs. Kennedy had forgotten her question to Lois. Lois didn't want to answer her mother. She didn't want to admit that some of the kids had been listening to Thekla's muttered speculations. They were wondering if Mayor Timothy Grass should be brought in for questioning.

But brought in by whom? He was the mayor.

At Thekla Mustard's house, Dr. Mustard paused after the evening toast and peered fondly at his wife and daughter. "You had a good day?" he asked the table at large.

Thekla was used to answering such questions, since all three Mustards knew they weren't meant for Mrs. Mustard, whose days were unvaryingly dull. But Thekla didn't feel like answering today. How could the day be good?

"Haven't you heard, Father," said Thekla in a neutral voice, "that my teacher has gone missing in action?"

"Oh, yes. Miss Earth," said Dr. Mustard. "Of course. I trust the excellent principal, Dr. Buttle, was able to summon a substitute? You wouldn't want to lose a valuable day of schooling if you hope to live a life rich in virtue and satisfaction."

"More baloney, dear?" said Mrs. Mustard in a strained voice, though in fact she hadn't served first helpings yet, and the meal wasn't even baloney—it was roast pork with sauerkraut and beets.

Thekla thought about Mayor Grass and what she'd overheard that day: "I'll always remember you like this.

113

Don't leave me." What if Miss Earth had done just that? And what if Mayor Grass, that calm, sweet man, *had* been driven mad with grief and committed a crime? She hated to think the worst of people. But maybe *someone* had to. And she was the only one who had eavesdropped on their conversation.

At the old Munning Mansion, where the Tweed family lived, there was no discussion about the disappearance of Miss Earth at all. Thud came home, but the house was cold, and the only lights lit were those on automatic timers. Harold had driven Mildred Tweed to the airport in Manchester, New Hampshire, to launch her latest whirlwind tour as Petunia Whiner.

Thud had given up on the notion of ratting on the Tattletales. Who cared, really? Let Sammy Grubb believe in a Missing Link out there somewhere. Maybe Sammy was happier thinking there was a mysterious unknown figure out in the world, waiting for him.

Thud made himself a sandwich of cheese, ham, pickles, salsa, mayonnaise, ketchup, and green olives, then threw it in the trash compactor because he wasn't hungry. He strummed air guitar for a while, pretending to play backup in his mother's band. Then he went to put in a video. He was going to watch the remake of *Planet of the Apes,* but the video in the machine was a tape of Petunia Whiner's Southern Comfort Tour several years back. He found himself watching it, winding and rewinding to the beginning, where Petunia Whiner first stormed the stage. In the background backstage, hardly visible, a kind of Missing Link of its own, was the silhouetted head of his father, Mycroft Tweed. He was smiling and clapping up a storm like the thousands of other fans, swept away in a kind of mass hysteria of devotion for Petunia Whiner.

Petunia Whiner—so different from Mildred Tweed! She was a strange monstrous creature in a fluorescent red wig, another kind of Missing Link in Thud's life.

She and his father both, pursuing their careers—concert halls and prison terms—with gusto and single-mindedness.

It hurt to be a human, really, thought Thud.

13

Where Were You That Day?

She struggled in a kind of sleep-drenched darkness—
no more than a limb turned this way, then that, or
an eyelid fluttering. There was resistance on every side,
and dark clamminess. She couldn't muster the concen-
tration to decide if the clamminess was within her head
or outside her before the waves of nausea returned and
she lapsed into senselessness.

On Thursday morning, Miss Earth had been missing for
over sixty hours. Her students, dragging themselves into
her classroom, were therefore hardly surprised to see
someone they had met a few weeks earlier—Vermont
State Trooper Hiram Crawdad.

"Kids," said Grandma Earth, who accompanied him,
"I don't need to tell you I'm mighty worried about

116

what's happened to my daughter, Germaine. She's gotten herself into some pickles before, but she's a thoughtful person. She always calls home if she's had a change of plans. Her fiancé, our first selectman, Timothy Grass, hasn't a clue as to her whereabouts. I know nothing, either. Therefore we've decided to call in a law enforcement professional. Maybe some of you know something that will be of use, even if you don't realize it. So please, I'm going to ask you to think, and to think hard and carefully, in answering Trooper Crawdad's questions. My daughter's well-being might depend on it."

Grandma Earth sat down at her daughter's desk, which as usual was neat and tidy. Trooper Crawdad cleared his throat and twisted his hands and made an attempt to look competent.

"Okay, kiddos," he said. "First things first. Do any of you know where your teacher might be, or where she went?"

The children sat and tried to think anew about it, as if they hadn't just spent the last forty-eight hours considering exactly that.

No one raised a hand for a moment. Then, despite the horrific nature of the situation, the kids' imaginations began to go into hyperdrive. Naturally. They'd been trained well, and by a very fine teacher indeed.

"Maybe Miss Earth decided to become a member of the corps de ballet in New York City or Paris or Sheboygan," suggested Sharday Wren, who took tap, jazz, and modern on successive afternoons. "You go, girl. Shake that booty."

"Might Miss Earth have taken a trip to Brattleboro or Hanover and, well, gotten lost?" said Fawn Petros, whose sense of direction wasn't the keenest.

"I think Miss Earth may have wanted to see some good avant-garde political theater in Greenwich Village," said Hector Yellow. "I wish I could have joined her."

"Far be it from me to cast aspersions on a fellow citizen," said Thekla Mustard, in a voice not of an empress but of a citizen. A voice, that is, suffused with hesitation and worry, not conviction. "Nevertheless, I can't help but wonder about our own Timothy Grass, commonly known as mayor, though in fact merely a selectman of this our humble village."

The room fell silent. Grandma Earth looked puzzled and irritated. "What leads you to say this, Thekla?"

Thekla didn't know if she was obliged to disclose that she'd eavesdropped on a conversation between Miss Earth and Mayor Grass. She never liked to reveal her tactics and strategies. But this wasn't a court of law, after all, only a classroom. Maybe common innuendo and hearsay were enough.

"Mayor Grass is a fine man, and we all like him," said Thekla at last, "but, Miss Earth being so lovable and all, perhaps *someone else* has come along to sweep our teacher off her feet. And maybe Mayor Grass—well, maybe he lost his cool. Forgot his manners."

Trooper Crawdad puffed out his cheeks and clamped his upper lip upon his lower in a way that suggested he himself might have been so tempted, though of course Trooper Crawdad was law-abiding as well as constitutionally too shy even to make friends with a puppy from the pound.

"*Nonsense,*" barked Grandma Earth. "If someone swept Germaine Earth off her feet, it was against her wishes. She loved—I mean she loves—Tim Grass. I won't hear a word said against him."

But there *were* words to say against him. Thekla's remark raised suspicions. In any unsolved crime, professional sleuths always have to consider the most likely party. Had Miss Earth and Mayor Grass quarreled? Had Mayor Grass become angry and struck her, and maybe—oh, terrible thought—even done her such damage that he'd had to hide her while she recuperated?

Hide her—or hide her corpse?

"Let's not go there," said Trooper Crawdad, seeing by the looks on the kids' faces where their minds were all going. "Back to my original question. Anything out of the ordinary happen around here this week?"

"Well, of course, there's always the Missing Link," said Sammy Grubb. "Maybe it got her."

"The Missing Link?" said Trooper Crawdad.

Sammy explained. The other boys chimed in. The girls fell portentously silent. Thekla Mustard sat up straight and kept her hands folded primly in the very very *very* center of her desktop. She was hugely pleased not to be the Empress at this moment.

When Sammy was done, Trooper Crawdad looked at Grandma Earth. "Any truth to this bunkum?"

"The kids have been talking about it for some time," admitted Grandma, "but Vermont kids can be suggestible. I suppose the grownups hereabouts have been humoring them. No one has put much stock in that nonsense."

Humoring them! Even the girls, who had arranged the April Fool's joke, were incensed.

But desperate situations require desperate measures, including honesty. So, in this instance, Thekla Mustard decided to be totally honest on behalf of the Tattletales, especially if it would make that stinker Lois Kennedy the Third look bad.

"There is no Missing Link," declared Thekla loudly. "Ask Lois. It was just an idea of hers, a ruse to dupe the boys. The Missing Link was really Thud Tweed in a gorilla suit rented from the Ethantown Mall."

You could have heard a pin drop. You could have heard a pin thinking, I'd like to hear a person drop for a change. Sammy Grubb's face turned an unusual color, part yellow, part beige, and he blinked more rapidly than the class was used to seeing him do. Traitors at every turn, he thought.

His fellow Copycats came to his rescue. "I can't believe it," said Moshe Cohn. "Treason on the part of Thud Tweed? It's not to be borne, by God."

"You meathead," said Stan Tomaski. "What a meathead you are, Thud. You meathead."

"I was going to explain!" said Thud. "At first I went along with it for a joke, but then I decided I was going to tell you about it. Really. You Copycats could play some further trick on the girls. I left a note for Sammy Grubb to meet me so I could tell him all about it, but he never showed up."

"This is getting us nowhere," said Trooper Crawdad. "Play your schoolyard tricks on your own time, young citizens. We have a missing teacher to locate."

"I never got any note from you," muttered Sammy. "You're a liar as well as a traitor. You could have just called me on the phone if you'd wanted to tell me something."

Lois was sending Thekla Mustard such dark looks of hatred that if Trooper Crawdad had not been wiping the corner of his eye with his handkerchief, he'd have put Lois under surveillance for possible intent to do Thekla grievous bodily harm.

Grandma Earth began to hunt through Miss Earth's desk drawers. She pulled out long chains of paper clips, boxes of gummed stars, stacks of assignments bound in rubber bands, and a paperback copy of Stephanie Queen's bestseller *Shanghaied in Shanghai*. On the cover was a picture of the heroine of the series, Spangles O'Leary, trying to escape from a fretwork of ropes and chains; she appeared to be padlocked to the green jaws of a leering dragon carved out of jade.

"Hey, I never read that one," said Trooper Crawdad. "Is it any good?"

"Hello," said Grandma Earth in a funny voice. "What do we have here?"

She had begun flipping through Miss Earth's lesson plan book. In the front of it, slipped under the acetate cover, was a piece of paper. Peering over the old woman's shoulder, Trooper Crawdad read along with her.

Hey, want to know who's on your side? Meet me in Foggy Hollow an hour after school gets out, and I'll let you in on a secret.

"I think we've hit pay dirt," said Trooper Crawdad. He took a sandwich bag from his pocket and shook out some crumbs, and then, holding only the corner of the note, he gently dropped it inside.

"What is it?" asked Sammy Grubb. All the kids craned to see, but nobody could make out what was on the scrap of paper.

"Confidential, that's what it is," said Trooper Crawdad.

"Anything else, kids?" asked Grandma Earth in a quavering voice.

"If it wasn't a Missing Link," said Thud Tweed sullenly, "maybe it was outer-space aliens. Or pirates on a ski vacation. Or giant blind moles who emerged from their earthen tunnels and mistook Miss Earth for a toothsome grasshopper."

"Don't get smart, you," said Trooper Crawdad.

"Yes, *sir*," answered Thud in a mocking manner.

Grandma Earth left the room without saying goodbye. Trooper Crawdad made a routine investigation of the rest of Miss Earth's desk and cupboard, but no other clues turned up. Then Mrs. Brill, the lunch lady, came in to supervise for the day.

"Let's compute the caloric contents of our lunches, shall we?" she said. The class groaned and got out their lunches. Before they'd gone halfway through the exercise, most of the kids had eaten their assignments, though it was hardly nine A.M., and so Mrs. Brill had to think of something else to do.

"Where were you between three P.M. and sunset on April fourth?"

At sunset on April 7, State Trooper Hiram Crawdad was posing this question to every citizen of Hamlet who came into Clumpett's General Store in the center of town.

"I have an airtight alibi. Just ask Gladys Petros. I was having my hair done at the Hamlet House of Beauty!" said Widow Wendell, shaking her coronet of gray ringlets at him. "Can't you tell? Doesn't it show? By the way, are you married?"

"That's confidential, miss," said Trooper Crawdad, and turned to Bucky and Olympia Clumpett.

"We were right here, Hi," said the Clumpetts, who had become chummy with the trooper following the affair of the three rotten eggs the month before. "Ringing up everyone's supper groceries, same as ever."

"I was in the library," said Mr. Dewey. "When I wasn't checking out books, I was standing at the Q shelf, reshelving Stephanie Queen novels. She's so popular."

"What do you think about *Shanghaied in Shanghai*?" asked Trooper Crawdad.

"I prefer *Loose in London* myself," said Mr. Dewey.

"That's the one where Spangles O'Leary falls in with a crowd of improvisational comedians who take over Scotland Yard for a lark. Essential professional reading for an officer of the law, I'd say." Trooper Crawdad took a note.

"What do you mean where was I?" Grandma Earth was incensed when Trooper Crawdad posed his question. "I was at the Baked Goods and Auto Repair Shop, of course, waiting for Germaine to come home. Where else would I be?"

"Sorry," said Trooper Crawdad. "Just doing my job."

"Well, do it better than that!"

Trooper Crawdad got embarrassed. The next person through the door was Thud Tweed. "Where were you between three P.M. and sunset on April fourth?" he asked Thud.

Thud didn't want to answer. He had been in Foggy Hollow, of course, waiting for Sammy Grubb to show up, and Harold could swear to it. But Thud had seen neither hide nor hair of Miss Earth. Foggy Hollow was extensive. The channel cut by the old stream was deep and winding and overgrown with young trees, so it was possible Miss Earth had been near and nonetheless he hadn't run into her. But Thud didn't want the whole store to hear he'd been hanging out in the very place where Miss Earth was presumed to have disappeared.

125

And luckily, Harold had been called out of town suddenly due to a family illness, so Thud was safe from discovery.

"I was home minding my own business. What's it to ya?" he muttered.

Thud was a big kid, but Trooper Crawdad didn't like being sassed. "I suppose your parents will corroborate your statement?" he said, just a tad threateningly.

"If you're going to get personal," said Thud loudly, "since everyone else already knows it, I'll tell you that my dad can't corroborate a thing. He's in jail for embezzlement."

"Immaterial to the matter at hand," said Trooper Crawdad with professional detachment. "Your mom available to interview?"

"Only if you're a member of the entertainment press corps," said Thud. "As you'll remember, she's the singer known as Petunia Whiner. America's Songbird has flown the coop to go on a tour."

"So who is your guardian while she's gone?"

"Supposed to be Harold, the butler/chauffeur. But he got an emergency message that his old dad broke a hip and several metatarsals falling out of a wheelchair. He had to fly to Palm Beach. Anyway, do I look like I need a guardian?" Thud Tweed swelled up to his fullest slabbed-out size.

Trooper Crawdad was not intimidated. "Oh, my boy," he said, "you certainly do look as if you need a guardian. I'm afraid we're going to have to make some arrangements with the Vermont Department of Social Services. You're still a minor. You can't stay under your own recognizance. I'm afraid you'll have to get in the cruiser."

"Trooper Crawdad," said Grandma Earth, coming back from the meat counter with a couple of pounds of pork sausages, "if it's all the same to you, why don't you release him to me?"

"I'm sure I'll need authorization from my superior officer, or from one of his parents," said Trooper Crawdad. "Besides, don't you have enough on your mind as it is?"

"It'll calm my nerves to have someone else in the house while my Germaine is missing. And lout though he looks, Thud isn't a bad sort. No reason to punish him for the shenanigans of his parents."

"Well, I'll have to check with headquarters," said Trooper Crawdad, not quite convinced.

"Use your cell phone. Work it out. I'll wait. Meanwhile, Thud, you can go sit in the truck," said Grandma. "We still have fifteen dozen doughnuts to bake for tomorrow morning's coffee hour."

Trooper Crawdad, intimidated by Grandma Earth,

fussed with his cell phone, dropped it, picked it up, and accidentally dialed Time and Temperature. When Thekla Mustard came in to buy a cabbage, he took the chance to reassert his professional nature. "Where were you between three P.M. and sunset on April fourth?" he demanded loudly of her.

"Where was Mayor Grass?" retorted Thekla. "Have you asked *him* yet?"

She spoke as quietly as she could, but the room had just fallen silent. Every word echoed off the glass doors of the refrigerator cases with a brittle, accusatory clarity.

"Guess I better go talk to Mayor Grass," said Trooper Crawdad with a sigh.

14

Beatrice Breaks Out

Thud Tweed did as he was told. He waited in the truck. After a few moments, Grandma Earth emerged from Clumpett's. Small and pluglike, Grandma Earth moved in a beetling sort of way, her hands gently pawing the air and her elbows pumping. She looked like a toddler in pajamas with feet, trying to get some purchase on a polished floor. As she climbed up into the driver's seat, Thud felt stiff and adult in an uncomfortable way. He was about twice as big as she.

And how odd, come to think of it, to be released into the custody of a teacher's *mother*! Thud had made enemies of teachers in Swiss boarding schools, in Virginia military academies, in Jesuit establishments, and in public schools the world over. He'd spent a summer at a fat camp once, trying to provoke the camp counselors into fits of anxious overeating. But never in his checkered career had a teacher just plain vanished on him.

Thud was sure that Miss Earth's disappearance would prove to be his fault. He just didn't know how.

It seemed odd to be heading somewhere other than home. Not that home felt very homey. The old Munning Mansion up on Squished Toad Road, which the Tweeds had bought earlier in the spring, had belonged to granite czar and local philanthropist Cornelius Munning. It was a pretentious pile of granite columns, Greek pediments, and Federal-style windows. Set in a landscape patchwork of walled gardens and reflecting pools, the mansion's spruce-lined lanes drew the eye to distant obelisks, wayward cows, and other romantic vistas.

You could not say it was a warm and cozy home.

The house where Sybilla Earth lived with her daughter, Germaine, on the other hand, was a simple board-and-batten cottage. The roof was steeply pitched to handle excessive snows, and the lathe-turned gingerbread was limited, in the frugal Vermont way, to a few modest scrollwork brackets supporting the eaves. The front porch, glassed in during the 1940s, made a small, bright room for tables and chairs. Here, customers of

Grandma Earth's Baked Goods and Auto Repair Shop could nibble on doughnuts while Grandma Earth finished overhauling alternators or replacing timing belts.

When Thud followed Grandma Earth into the shop, he thought of all the times Hamlet kids had burst through the door and pounded to the counter for their afterschool doughnuts. He felt both privileged and imprisoned when Grandma Earth said, "Don't be shy; the kitchen is here behind the counter. I trust you can follow basic instructions?"

"*I* wouldn't trust me," said Thud.

"We'll go slow," said Grandma Earth. "As the lady said, 'Stand facing the stove. . . .'" She was putting on an apron, and she threw one across the room to Thud.

"I can't wear this!"

"Why, too small?"

"It's an apron. It's—it's beyond wimpy."

"Think of it as a surgeon's gown."

Thud floundered. "You'll tip me into a lather of gender confusion!"

"If you're that easily tipped, sonny, you better get used to it now. Gee, but you're a big fellow." The apron barely covered Thud's front, and the apron strings could be tied with only the smallest of bows. "Now measure out twenty-four cups of best unbleached flour into the mixing bowl." Grandma Earth pointed to a tub the size of a bassinet.

"Anyone comes in here and sees me cooking, I'll lose all credibility," said Thud.

"You don't have that much to start with," said Grandma Earth, "so don't worry about it." She turned on Vermont Public Radio to see if there was any late-breaking news about a Missing Link or a missing teacher. VPR was sadly silent on both subjects.

Hamlet citizens, proud of Miss Earth and protective of her mother, did not know what to say to Sybilla Earth about the disappearance of her daughter. No one wanted to suspect Tim Grass, but how could you not *wonder*?

So nobody came to buy baked goods that evening, not a single customer. Grandma Earth shut down early, fed Thud some pork sausages, and showed him the guest room.

He went to bed with the door open, listening to the wheeze and mutter of Grandma Earth, who eventually laid her body down on top of the blankets of her own bed. She rested, unable to sleep, keenly sensing the unfamiliar loneliness in the house.

On Friday morning Miss Earth had been missing for three and a half days. It was impossible not to gossip anymore. Any grudge that anyone in town had ever had against anyone else was aired—not just in the privacy of homes, where such remarks were made supposedly in confidence, but also in the public clearinghouse of the schoolyard, where the same remarks were repeated with gusto, fear, and an intention to impress.

Stan Tomaski said, "My mom thinks Widow Wendell did away with Miss Earth because the widow wants to marry Tim Grass herself."

Fawn Petros said, "Hank McManus at my mom's beauty salon said Miss Earth wanted an especially curly perm last weekend. He thinks this shows that she *was* meeting a new boyfriend somewhere."

"She could have wanted to impress her fiancé even more, to win him back!" said Carly Garfunkel loyally. "My sister Paula guesses that Mayor Grass had his eye on someone else and wanted to get Miss Earth out of the way!"

"It couldn't have been Mayor Grass!" said Fawn Petros. "He wouldn't harm a flea. He wouldn't harm a microbe. He wouldn't reduce a fraction to its lowest common denominator."

"Well, does anyone know what Mayor Grass's alibi is for Monday evening?" asked Forest Eugene Mopp.

Anna Maria Mastrangelo said, "He says he left work early because he'd injured his hand while he was putting away the cement mixer. His hand is in a bandage, apparently."

"But is that the real reason?" said Thekla. "Maybe Miss Earth put up a struggle. . . ."

"He couldn't have hurt Miss Earth!" said Sammy Grubb stoutly.

"Maybe it was the Missing Link," said Fawn. Her classmates explained again to her that the Missing Link had been a hoax that she, in fact, had taken part in perpetrating. "Oh, right," she said.

"Maybe one of the six haunted hairdos returned and spirited Miss Earth off to the land of make-believe," said Mike Saint Michael, scoffing. "I mean, let's stay *real* here, folks."

"If she died," said Sharday Wren, "do you think her ghost would stay with us to see us through the rest of the school year anyway?"

No one could answer this question. It was too silly and too terrible at the same time. Luckily just then Mrs. Cobble joined the teachers in the lineup to usher the students of the Josiah Fawcett Elementary School into their classrooms.

"Well, we're taking turns helping out," said Mrs. Cobble, standing gingerly behind Miss Earth's desk, "and it's my turn. I don't have much to offer you kiddos.

I'm just the lowly secretary. But I'll do my part, in fond memory of Miss Earth." She looked as if she was about to cry.

"We'll listen, Mrs. Cobble," said Sammy Grubb in a soft voice.

The other children murmured in assent.

She cleared her throat. "Good. Well, school secretaries have only one skill, really, when you come right down to it. Today we're going to go in right up to our keisters into disaster-management training. DO YOU HEAR ME! I SAID DO YOU HEAR ME!"

"Yes Mrs. Cobble! We hear you Mrs. Cobble!"

"I CAN'T HEAR YOU! I SAID DO YOU HEAR ME!"

"YES MRS. COBBLE!" they screamed. "EVERY WORD MRS. COBBLE!"

"INCOMING!" shouted Mrs. Cobble. "HIT THE FLOOR!"

Sixteen students dove from their desks and flattened themselves on the linoleum. The corner of the room where Thud sat shook harder than the rest. Even Kermit the Hermit, the class frog, hit the colored pebbles of his terrarium.

"MOPP!" bellowed Mrs. Cobble. "TRIAGE QUESTION! YOU GOT A BLOODY NOSE ON THE

PLAYGROUND, UPSET TUMMIES IN THE KINDERGARTEN, FLASH FIRE IN THE CAFETE-RIA STEAM COUNTER, AND THE CHECKS FOR THE PHONE BILL HAVE JUST BOUNCED! WHADDYA HANDLE FIRST?"

Forest Eugene Mopp couldn't speak. He couldn't even look up from the floor. Neither he nor anyone else in the room had ever seen this side of Mrs. Cobble before.

"MUSTARD!"

Thekla Mustard leaped to her feet. "PERMISSION TO ASK FOLLOW-UP QUESTION SIR!"

"DENIED! THE FIRE'S JUST SPREAD TO THE SALAD BAR WHILE YOU DITHER! GRUBB!"

Sammy Grubb leaped to his feet. "HANDLE THE FIRE FIRST SIR!"

"WRONG!" Mrs. Cobble's eyes flashed. "KENNEDY!"

Lois Kennedy the Third leaped to her feet. "PAY THE PHONE BILL SIR!"

"RIGHT! WHY!"

"I HAVE NO IDEA SIR!"

Mrs. Cobble's eyes shone with tears. In her usual calm, quiet voice she remarked, "My husband, the fire chief, reminds me constantly. In a crisis, you must keep

136

your lines of communication open at all times, duckies. You need the phone to call the fire department, the doctor, and the police. Besides, you never know when dear Miss Earth might be phoning in. She could be in distress and need help."

The kids climbed back into their seats, rattled. It was going to be a long day.

It was strange to feel so tired on such a beautiful afternoon, but Mrs. Cobble had kept them being all that they could be until they could hardly be anything at all. At the end of the day, Mrs. Cobble had put on a little lipstick, snapped her pocketbook shut, and commented spiritedly, "Well, that's what it's like being a school secretary, folks. A prior career in the United States military sure helps. Being a school secretary is a rewarding job, but it does take the mickey out of you."

"Yes, sir," they mumbled.

Like a squadron of survivors after a long day of battle, Miss Earth's students left the school without speaking, without looking at each other, but without wanting to split up either. No one actually said, "Let's go hang out at Old Man Fingerpie's farm." But the students had a general interest in the well-being of their secret Flameburper. At least it gave them a common sense of purpose during this difficult period of waiting. Thud was expected at Grandma Earth's right after school for doughnut detail, but he had no intention of rushing. Everyone ended up trudging up the slopes of Squished Toad Road except Pearl Hotchkiss, who had to babysit.

Flossie Fingerpie was transferring flats of seedlings into the garden. "You think we're truly over the last frost?" she asked the kids. "I got these lovely little squash plants started in the parlor in February, and I've been making them hardy on the back porch. Think they're ready?"

"Be all you can be," said Sammy Grubb to a squash seedling.

"Let me know what you think about your little Beatrice in there," said Flossie. "She's going through another phase, I think. She goes through stages the way Old Man Fingerpie goes through denture-rinse tablets."

They entered the barn with a vague sense of unease. It took a moment for their eyes to adjust to the gloom. Doozy Dorking was perched on the half wall of a horse stall, looking down suspiciously into the whelping pen. The kids peered in the same direction.

Beatrice the Flameburper had enlarged her little cocoon. The kids could hear her inside it, clucking irritably to herself. Roughly the size of a porcupine, the cocoon rolled around like a bewitched vacuum cleaner bag.

"Nice little condo she's built around herself," said Flossie, coming into the barn for a trowel. "She's been in there since you left on Wednesday evening. Have no idea why. I think something's stalking the farm at night—something big. And she senses it. She's scared out of her pinfeathers."

"You have a dog for protection, don't you?" asked Lois.

"Cassius is deafer than Old Man himself, and he has amnesia," said Flossie. "He forgets to wake up."

"Doozy stands guard, I bet," said Mike. "Don't you, Doozy?"

"Doozy don't know what to do," said Flossie. "Oooh, lookee, the pack of straw is shaking and rolling. Beatrice must be waking up. She's been still as a stone for over a day. Thought she might be dead."

As if on cue, the cocoon began to wobble even more ferociously.

"I get the feeling we've seen Beatrice do this once before," said Lois to Thud. They both had watched the three rotten eggs hatch some weeks earlier.

Suddenly one end of the cocoon burst into flames. Doozy Dorking gave a strangled sort of cluck and leaped straight up, hitting her head against a beam and tumbling backward into the horse stall. Sammy Grubb shouted, "Keep the lines of communication open!" Lois Kennedy the Third shouted, "Hit the dirt!" But there was too much muck from unfastidious animals lying about, so no one obeyed her. Calmly, Flossie Fingerpie turned the spigot of the newly laid water pipe and prepared a bucket for dousing the flames.

But the fire died down without catching on the whole cocoon, and out wriggled Beatrice.

Only it wasn't Beatrice anymore—or not the Beatrice they had known.

Beatrice no longer looked anything like a chick, except for the funny sprig of green feathers that had graced her head in infancy. Her neck had lengthened. As she squirmed through the tight shoulders of the cocoon wrapping, the last of her downy pinfeathers were scraped away, and the skin underneath was a swamp green with an iridescence of turquoise about it. It was leathery like a lizard's skin, and Beatrice's lidded eyes looked cheapened by a bluish liner. Her genes had reverted to blue-toe lizard somewhat, though she still had small wings scrunched like epaulets over her front legs. When she opened her mouth to breathe, she squawked, a sound not unlike Doozy Dorking's.

"*Squawk?*" said Doozy Dorking in return, from the horse stall.

"Land o' Goshen," said Flossie Fingerpie. "Beatrice has given herself a makeover. Now she's into leather." She opened the door of the whelping pen to dash a bucket of water over the gently smoldering cocoon.

Doozy Dorking, who had managed to flutter to the top of the wall again, clucked in stepchickenly disapproval at Beatrice's new look.

By the time Thud Tweed got back to Grandma Earth's, she was halfway through the doughnut detail herself. She didn't complain that he was late. She tied his apron on him and told him to take over the deep-frying. "Two messages for you," she said in a terse voice. "Number one: Your mother has agreed that you may stay here until her tour is over or until I toss you out, whichever comes first. Number two: Sammy Grubb called to say Forest Eugene's dog, Migraine, appears to have been attacked by a coydog or some other creature."

"Oh, poor Forest Eugene," said Thud.

"Yes, and poor Migraine," said Grandma Earth, "but the dog will make it, they think."

After a few dozen doughnuts, Thud thought to say, "Did you have any messages for yourself today?"

"Didn't know you cared," said Grandma Earth, allowing herself that much sarcasm. But she pulled herself together and added, "No further clues on the whereabouts of my daughter. I hear that Mayor Tim Grass has been detained for questioning by Vermont state troopers, however."

Her voice was very cool and even. Thud couldn't tell if it was because she was glad Mayor Grass was being questioned or furious about it. Or just irked at Thud for being late.

Thud made the rest of the doughnuts without a word. When the last rack was set out to cool and be iced, Grandma Earth pulled two pizzas from the oven. She cut each one in half and tossed half of one in the garbage.

"What'd you do that for?" he asked.

"You worked roughly half the time I needed you for," she said, "so you get half the food. You want time off, arrange it ahead of time so I can plan my workday better."

"Waste of food," he said.

"Waste of time, waste of breath, waste of energy," she answered. She poured him half a glass of milk, poured herself a whole glass, and held her glass out toward his. "Cheers, Thud."

He picked up his glass and considered thudding it so

hard against hers that both glasses would shatter. But Grandma Earth seemed shattered enough, he decided. So he just drank his half glass of milk.

She's worried Mayor Grass is the cause of her daughter's disappearance, and she hates herself for it, he thought. She's taking it out on me. I can deal.

But he could think of nothing to say to comfort her.

15

Mrs. Mustard Breaks Out

The weekend began horribly and continued worse. To start with, the weather was lousy. Harsh rains pelted the uplands, the woodlands, the wetlands, the blacktopped roads, the stubbly meadows, and the shingled roofs. The downpour crushed the rain hats of Hamlet citizens who had joined Vermont state troopers in trying to comb every cranny and nook within the town borders. Volunteer firefighters from nearby Ethantown, Chumptown Falls, Puster Center, and Crank's Corners joined in too. But you could hardly see as far as your hand. The rain turned every near object into a silver silhouette. Farther features, like barn silos or the brow of Hardscrabble Hill, were lost to view entirely.

Friends and neighbors set up a relief station in the basement of the Congregational/Unitarian Church.

Grandma Earth and Thud Tweed had been working since five A.M. to prepare doughnuts and coffee for wet volunteers. Salim Bannerjee's dad contributed eight gallons of chicken vindaloo and enough rice to fill a cement mixer. Father Fogarty and Forest Eugene's mother, the Reverend Mrs. Mopp, chatted with worried citizens, and all day long Salim ladled rice and splashed chicken vindaloo onto paper plates, whether people wanted it or not.

Salim had said he didn't want to be there. The thought of anything bad happening to Miss Earth made him squeamish. But his dad had insisted, and now Salim found that he was glad. It felt good to do *something,* even if it was just a little vindaloo therapy.

Principal Buttle and the county sheriff had decided that children were not allowed to join the search-and-rescue teams. Naturally they protested. "She's *our* teacher!" cried Lois Kennedy the Third.

"Listen to me," said Lois's mother. "How much good would it do anyone to have some well-meaning child slip down a muddy gully and brain herself on a rock in the bottom of one of these torrential streams?"

Other parents held the same notion, more or less. The children were outnumbered. But Sammy Grubb's dad had left early to do a drywall job over in Forbush Corners, and his mom was trying to pick up some extra small change by selling homemade potholders at the weekly tailgate tag sale in the lot next to the Mobil station in Sharon. So by the time Sammy woke up, there was no one to nix any bright ideas he might have.

He didn't go out right away. The first thing he did was make a cup of hot water with milk in it, to warm up. Then he took down the drawings and the reference material of the many monsters he had hoped to find someday. He heaped them together under his bed. It made him feel young and stupid to have cared so much—to have cared so very much—about something as silly as a Missing Link.

I should have gotten up earlier and gone with Dad, he thought. Drywalling would have been a sad waste of a Saturday. But adult life means putting crazy dreams of monsters aside. Might as well get used to it.

But he had slept too late, thanks to crazy dreams of monsters. His dad was gone already, and so was his mom, and the house was quiet and chilly.

So he pulled on his sweatshirt and his denim jacket and jammed a Red Sox cap on his head, and pushed out into the rain.

Off the back stoop, once you cleared the spare car parts, you came to a pair of old maple trees that more or less supported Sammy's treehouse. Climbing the sagging, tired limbs was like climbing the spokes of a huge blown-out umbrella. Since there was a roof on the treehouse, Sammy could keep somewhat dry as he peered down the slope that ran behind the house into Foggy Hollow.

He could make out four or five yellow hunched shapes. People were poking sticks into thickets of bracken, calling "Germaine? Germaine Earth?" Sammy saw one hardy soul go nearly waist-deep into the swollen stream, to prod the muddy bottom with a stout staff. The hood fell back when the searcher pulled herself out of the muck. It was the school nurse, Pinkella Crisp. Her face was worn and crumpled.

Sammy ran down to her and asked for an update. She couldn't speak for a moment, catching her breath. "I'm still new to this part of Vermont, Sammy—as you know. I moved here only last fall. I had no idea these badlands were so thickly overgrown. At least they're not in full leaf yet—but heavens to Betsy Ross, a body could roll into a thicket and never be found."

He didn't bother to offer to help. He didn't waste his breath. He knew very well what line any responsible adult would take. So he watched Nurse Crisp rejoin her team, and then he headed into the village.

Overshooting the eastern edge of the village green, he stopped at Grandma Earth's to get a doughnut for breakfast. Grandma was in one of the repair bays, looking at a state trooper's car, which had been stalling out.

Thud lurked behind the counter, squirting raspberry jam into doughnut pouches.

"Nice apron, bakery boy," said Sammy. "After you're finished with it, may I have it? I can make a tent for my whole family as well as a dozen of our nearest relatives."

"Don't be a jerk, you jerk," said Thud.

"You're the jerk," said Sammy. "You're the traitor. *Traitor.* How *could* you throw your lot in with the Tattletales? How could you embarrass the boys in your class? And make a fool of me?"

"I didn't invent that stupid fight between the Tattletales and the Copycats," said Thud. "You all signed on to that war long before I showed up."

"But I'm your friend," said Sammy. "Or I was."

"Look, I'm sorry," said Thud. "Give me a break, will you? After all, once I saw how embarrassed you were, I tried to think of a way to make it up to you. My April Fool's revenge trick."

"The Copycats had decided not to play a trick on the girls," said Sammy. "You knew that, Thud."

"I'm new in town. And I'm not a full-fledged Copycat. Frankly, I haven't had all that much practice at belonging to a club, except Detention Club at the Tough Love Summer Camp."

"Going to go all weepy on me?" said Sammy, though he regretted it as soon as he said it. Maybe Thud was actually telling the truth. "It's just so embarrassing. Tricked by a gorilla mask."

"Well, it was a high-quality mask. And I did do a good job hunching and leaping and growling. Grownups usually call me an animal anyway. For once I measured up.

"Besides," Thud continued, "I don't know why you're so prickly. You wanted to find a Missing Link. Isn't scaly old Beatrice enough of a monster for you? I mean, those weird wings, that hot breath, the front paws that are rather creepily like claws? Why do you need to find a gorilla-shaped Missing Link on top of it? Sometimes what life hands you has to be enough, you know. But everyone wants what they don't have. . . ."

"If you want friends, Thud, that's a heck of a way to make them."

"Live and learn," said Thud. He juggled a doughnut into the air and batted it across the counter at Sammy. In a little puff of powdered sugar, Sammy neatly caught it. It was a jelly-filled peace offering.

Sammy laughed and, for an instant, felt a little better. Thud laughed too, not so meanly as he sometimes could. But when Grandma Earth came in from the garage, they both took a look at how her chins were sagging with exhaustion and worry, and the moment of relief passed.

❀ ❀ ❀

On Sunday the rain continued, but with less force, so more people were out rambling along their property lines, looking for anything peculiar. The Clumpetts posted a notice on the bulletin board outside their store calling for a meeting in the Flora Tyburn Memorial Gym that evening at seven. By six fifty-five, parked cars stretched from the gym all the way back into the village.

The last time so many townspeople had been in the same place at the same time was when Petunia Whiner had given a benefit concert to raise money for the new fire engine. Then the mood had been jolly, even giddy. Now folks sat in folding chairs and dispensed with chitchat. They kept their arms folded over their coats. Old Man Fingerpie wobbled in with Flossie, sat down, and promptly fell asleep.

Hamlet had three selectmen. They were Tim Grass (called the mayor), Dr. Heidi Sternbaum, the pediatrician, and Clem Fawcett, the great-great-great-great-grandnephew of Josiah Fawcett, founder of Hamlet.

Thekla's worries about Tim Grass had circulated, and her fear had proved slightly infectious. Since Mayor Grass was under suspicion of foul play, few people expected him to attend. But no charges had been filed and no arrests made, and when the door opened and he came in, folks made a decent effort not to whisper. A deeper hush fell over the room, though.

"Hi, Tim," said folks near him. "Howdy. How's it going?" They didn't speak as if they expected an answer, and they got none.

Grandma Earth arrived and sat in the back with Thud Tweed. Other kids—not just Miss Earth's students, but middle school and high school kids too—made a showing here and there in the crowd. But there was none of the usual hollering that kids do.

Sammy Grubb was present. Thekla Mustard was there. Lois Kennedy the Third was too. Salim, Fawn, Hector, Pearl. Other kids.

Mayor Grass made his way to the front of the room and conferred briefly with Dr. Sternbaum and Clem Fawcett. Then he straightened up and said in a carrying voice, "This isn't the annual town meeting—that'll happen later. This is just—just us. So we have no rules of order to follow. The thought was just that we share what we know."

Olympia Clumpett stood up, and in her ammonia-and-shoe-polish voice, she brayed, "I'll get straight to the point, folks. Bucky and I asked for this meeting 'cause we didn't like the tone of the conversations we were overhearing at the store. Folks pointing fingers and muttering dirty rumors about each other. Chiefly 'bout our selectman and neighbor Tim Grass, to call a spade a spade."

People squirmed in their seats, bunched up their jacket collars, and muttered, but to themselves, not to Mayor Grass.

Trooper Crawdad was in the back of the room. He raised his hand and was recognized. "Matter of public record, folks: We took Timothy Grass in for fingerprinting because we located a document of suspicious origin. We lifted prints off it to compare them to Mayor Grass's."

Dimitri Petros called, "Of course they don't match. Do they?"

Mayor Grass lifted his right hand. It was bandaged. "I got my hand caught in the cement mixer crankshaft when I was cleaning out the thing following the pouring of new pavement over at the school. My fingers are scabbed over. So I couldn't be fingerprinted accurately."

"Anybody witness that, Tim?" called Flossie Fingerpie.

"Sorry, no. Hank and Otis had already gone home for the night."

"How convenient," whispered someone from the back of the room.

"And the typeface on the printed note is a standard face available in Microsoft Word," said Mayor Grass. "I'm the first to point this out. I have Word on my computer, like a lot of folks."

"This is a waste of our tax dollars. Waste of time!" called Mr. Dewey loyally. "Sit down, Tim! Nobody's pointing a finger!"

"Trooper Crawdad is right to pursue every lead," insisted Mayor Grass. "He's just doing his job."

"People are innocent until proven guilty," said Clem Fawcett. His tone was menacingly even. "But for the period in question, I'm guessing that Mayor Grass doesn't have an alibi that can be corroborated. Does he?" He turned to his fellow selectman.

Mayor Grass shrugged and then shook his head. "You know I live alone, Clem. Up over the Vermont Museum of Interesting Things to Know and Tell. After I hurt my hand, I went home and took some Bufferin for the pain and went to bed early. Didn't see anyone. Didn't phone anyone. That's the truth."

The room was silent but for the whip-whip of the ceiling fans, until Grandma Earth called out in irritation, "Trooper Crawdad! What *have* you discovered? Anything we should know about?"

"We have no reason to detain anyone just now," said Trooper Crawdad. "All we hear is gossip and innuendo. There's no evidence of foul play. Everyone knows we found Miss Earth's Kawasaki 8000 Silver Eagle motorcycle abandoned behind the library. But someone might have stolen the vehicle from Miss Earth and left it there to throw us off the scent."

"Are the rest of us in danger? What are we to do?" cried the Reverend Mrs. Mopp. "Besides pray, I mean?"

"A person's not considered missing, legally, until three days have passed," said Trooper Crawdad. "More than three days have passed. So we've put out a statewide bulletin. We're posting it on national Web sites as well. Sadly, we have very little to go on. Miss Earth seems well liked."

"Well *loved*!" shouted Widow Wendell.

There was a pause while the crowd considered the truth of this. Then everyone began to mumble about how wonderful Miss Earth was, really. Who could have done such a thing to her? The mood got just a little ugly.

Grandma Earth sensed what was going on. She stood up. "Let's deal with the necessaries before we commence with the eulogies or the posse. While we wait for a break in the case, what's happening in her classroom? Who's minding her students?"

Principal Buttle climbed on a folding chair so she could be heard. "We don't have much of a budget for substitute teachers," she said, "but state law requires us to educate our students whether their teachers have vanished or not. This past week the school staff took turns looking in, but we need to find a more permanent solution. Would anyone care to volunteer as a substitute teacher?"

Everyone stared at the floor.

"I'll volunteer!" roared Old Man Fingerpie, having just woken up. "What for?"

No one answered and he fell asleep again.

"Without a volunteer," said Principal Buttle, "I suppose I'll have to ask my other teachers to double up."

Thekla Mustard found herself on her feet. "If I may be allowed a moment to address the assembled citizens . . . ," she began.

"A moment or an hour?" murmured Sammy to Thud, which was his way of signaling, *Okay, I'm over it, Thud. Let's move on.*

". . . I would like to mention that it is humiliating to find that no one in town wants to teach us. We are fine students, some of us far above average. We think it would be a fitting memorial to Miss Earth that people carry on her good work."

"You make it sound as if she's croaked," said Jasper Stripe, wiping his nose.

"The thing is," said Clem Fawcett, "no one would dare step into Miss Earth's shoes. She is a very fine teacher; we all know that. No one could take her place."

"No one *can* ever take her place," agreed Thekla smoothly, "but not even to try would be to let her down. Surely someone will stand forward?"

In the back of the room, a figure with a bowed head

stood up. A voice sounded—timorously at first. In the crowd Thekla couldn't make out whose voice it was. Then she froze in disbelief.

"I'm not used to spending much time out of the house during the day," said the volunteer, "but perhaps this is a time for all of us to do something we're not used to. I'll pitch in for a time, if my help is needed."

Everyone turned. Everyone stared. The speaker was Thekla's mother, Mrs. Norma Jean Mustard.

16

Thud Tweed,
Juvenile Offender

"**H**ow kind of you, Mrs. Mustard," said Principal Buttle, looking this way and that. "I would have always assumed you were too—busy—to look in on the classroom."

"Housework *is* consuming if you do it right," admitted Norma Jean Mustard with a bit of a sigh. "Consuming, but not rewarding. So I'm ready to volunteer if there's no one else available. Even if it's only for a day or two. I'm sure it won't be more than that."

Thekla suspected that her father was home, snoring softly under a copy of *Ophthalmology Today*. What would he say about such an insult to tradition? Mrs. Mustard looked flushed, brave, and terrified all at once.

"We accept your offer," said Principal Buttle. "I'll

chat with you after the meeting and give you a ten-minute pep talk."

"Now that that's settled," said Dr. Sternbaum, "I want to call on Trooper Crawdad to share with us the text of the suspicious note that he recovered, the one that cast aspersions of guilt upon my fellow selectman Tim Grass."

"No can do," said Trooper Crawdad. "Headquarters is still scrutinizing it for hidden meanings."

"We might be better at figuring out hidden meanings, Trooper Crawdad." Dr. Sternbaum was used to giving shots to screaming children, and she shot Trooper Crawdad a look as if she might approach him with a spare hypodermic. He caved.

"Near as I can remember," he said, "it went something like this: 'Want to know who's on your side? Meet me in Foggy Hollow an hour after school gets out, and I'll let you in on a secret.'"

Thud Tweed froze in his seat. He'd had a feeling he was going to be implicated somehow. Now he knew how.

"We don't know what it means," said Trooper Crawdad.

"*I* sure don't know what it means," said Tim Grass. "It's true that I've taken to going for a walk with Miss Earth when she gets out of school. Especially now the weather is better. But I don't write notes like that."

"Not anymore," called someone from the back.

"'I'll let you in on a secret,' the note reads," Trooper Crawdad said. "I wonder what secret. Could it refer to the Missing Link creature in Foggy Hollow? That practical joke that the kids were playing on each other for April Fool's Day?"

"Is there a creature on the loose in Foggy Hollow?" asked Old Man Fingerpie, waking up again. "You mean like a bobcat, or a tax collector, or what?"

"Something scared my cows silly the other night!" called Abe Skillet from near the windows. "They smelled something they didn't like, or heard something they didn't care to hear. They broke down two stalls trying to move away from the door. And these are my special girls, my Lippizaner dancing cows. They tend to Quaker attitudes. They don't take against much."

"Something attacked my dog, Migraine, too!" called Forest Eugene Mopp. "It was a coyote, we think. Or a coydog."

"Something left odd tracks in the newly poured cement of the school pavement," said Tim Grass. "I thought it was the kids messing around again, but maybe it wasn't."

"Could it be that freakoid chick thing at Fingerpie Farm?" called Widow Wendell. "I don't like messing with Mother Nature!"

"That 'chick thing' is just going through a stage," said Flossie Fingerpie. "Beatrice may have the *so-what* attitude of a teenager, but she's only about as big as your brain, Wilma Wendell. She might think about bringing down a dog or scaring a herd of high-strung cows, but I doubt she could manage it. Besides, I don't let her have the run of the village. Let's not turn her into a scapegoat."

The back door banged open. It was Father Fogarty. "Sorry I'm late—I walked." He stamped the wet from his shoes and said, "You still fussing about Missing Links? Look what I just found under the highway bridge, where it crosses Foggy Hollow. It must have floated down the stream that's begun to cascade along that stretch. It fetched up between a couple of rocks and a tree trunk."

He held something up. Everyone began to scream. It was a person's head, made horrible with decay and rot.

Then someone began to snort with laughter, and the others caught on. It wasn't the head of Miss Earth. It was a waterlogged rubberized gorilla mask. Its cavernous nostrils were like the finger holes in a bowling ball—rain ran out freely.

It was good to laugh. The meeting broke up and conversation erupted as farmers started sharing tales about rogue dogs in their sheep fields and snapping turtles getting their ducks. Sammy Grubb noticed, however, that people gave Mayor Grass a little bit of a berth as they headed for the doors. Tim Grass stood with his bandaged hand in one pocket of his jacket, almost as if he didn't want anyone to remember it.

Thekla Mustard went and stood beside her mother, experiencing an odd insignificance. She'd never felt this way before, and for a moment, the novelty of it was engaging.

Grandma Earth's home and shop were only a few moments away from the Flora Tyburn Memorial Gym. Grandma Earth and Thud Tweed walked in single file along the side of the road, thinking dark and gloomy thoughts, but about different things.

"I believe Tim Grass when he says he didn't write that note," said Grandma Earth at last, as if trying to convince herself. "He's a busy fellow. He doesn't have time to go monkeying around with secrets and games. Besides, he respects Germaine's work far too much. He knows that being a teacher is a hard job, Thud. But who might have sent that wicked note to Germaine, luring her to some location where she might be kidnapped—or worse?"

Thud was glad of the April darkness. In a small voice he said, "Well, I might have."

They kept walking. Grandma Earth put one solid work boot in front of the other and waited until she was sure there were no other townspeople within hearing. Then she turned around. "Say that again, Thud?"

He didn't look her in the eye. He mumbled, "That note sounds an awful lot like one I wrote. But I didn't write it for Miss Earth, and I don't know how she got it. I wrote it for Sammy Grubb."

"Why?"

Thud explained. First he'd taken part in an April Fool's joke on the boys. Then he had wanted to double-cross the girls and confess to Sammy so they could plan a return April Fool's trick on the girls. Only it backfired, and somehow Miss Earth had come across the note. Perhaps she had thought it was meant for her.

"I suppose if Germaine thought she was going to meet someone in Foggy Hollow, then parking her motorcycle behind the library made sense. The Hamlet House of Beauty, Clumpett's General Store, the library—all those backyards slope down to Foggy Hollow sooner or later. But Thud, if you didn't do anything wrong, why didn't you speak up?"

"Do you believe that I didn't do anything wrong?" he asked.

"Why didn't you speak up?" asked Grandma Earth again, tersely.

"I have bad press," he said. "I came to town with a reputation as a juvenile delinquent, and I haven't done such a good job of turning over a new leaf. *I* know I didn't do anything wrong, but I also know people are always glad to have someone to blame. I'm big," he continued, "big for my age, and I'm meaner than you folks in Vermont tend to be. I'm a flatlander. I'm from away. Furthermore, my family is rich. You Hamlet folks don't have any reason to cut me any slack. I haven't given you any reason to trust me, really."

"No," said Grandma Earth, "you haven't. But as Germaine has pointed out to me many times, self-esteem isn't handed out by parents and teachers like gold stars or an allowance. A person has to earn self-esteem. You better start doing that, Thud. And you might start right now, by going and telling Trooper Crawdad what you know."

"Do I have to do it tonight?" he said.

"Thud!" barked Grandma Earth. "Are you nuts? My daughter is *missing*! I don't want Vermont state troopers wasting valuable time following false leads!"

"I see what you mean," he said. "I'll go right back." He turned on his heel and headed back toward the gym.

"Do you want me to come with you?" called Grandma Earth in a softer voice. He didn't answer, and she didn't follow him.

Thekla Mustard was still waiting while her mother discussed teaching methods with Principal Buttle. She saw Thud Tweed come back into the gym and hang around near Trooper Crawdad until he was done yakking with Bucky and Limpy Clumpett. Thekla saw Thud lower his head and shuffle his feet and mutter something to the law enforcement official. Then she saw Trooper Crawdad sigh and straighten his shoulders and frogmarch Thud into the cloakroom of the gym.

"He's done something bad—again," said Thekla. *"Boys."* But to her surprise, this didn't give her any kind of boost. When trouble was serious enough, it affected everyone. And Thekla was troubled for Thud.

17

Beware What You Choose

The Mustard house was dark except for a smear of golden light through the windows of the front room, where, Thekla and her mother both knew, Dr. Mustard would be sitting, thinking about life. Thekla could sense her mother's nervousness as Norma Jean Mustard removed the keys from the car and then sat there stiffly, thinking, no doubt, of what she was going to say to her husband.

They went inside. Thekla would have liked to go directly to her room, but her mother—her modest, quiet, untroubled mother—said in a conversational tone, "Let's tell your father our news, shall we?"

"*Our* news?" asked Thekla.

But she didn't abandon her mother. Lost in a world of her own devising so often, Thekla nonetheless had begun to notice recently how little stimulated by life her mother appeared. And since Thekla was at present a silent partner in the Tattletales Club, neither its Empress nor its foe, this gave her time to consider, just for a minute, anyway, the virtue of befriending her mother. Now, when she seemed to need it.

"You have *what*?" said Dr. Mustard, putting his newspaper down with a sudden snap.

"I've volunteered to pitch in and help in the classroom, starting tomorrow morning," said Mrs. Mustard. "It's the right thing to do, I think."

"Norma Jean! Charity is one thing—who can disapprove of it? But it doesn't suit a woman of your station to stand behind a desk and lecture children! I won't have it!"

"Josif, I have no station," said Mrs. Mustard. She sat down and put her hands in the lap of her coat, which she hadn't yet removed. "This isn't imperial Prussia. I'm a middle-class American housewife who spends far too much time washing the stickiness off spice jars. I have no delusions of grandeur. I have no ambitions except to be a good wife and mother. And yet I would like to help. It would do me good."

"I won't have you laboring like a scullery maid," said Dr. Mustard. "I trained in medicine so I could afford to keep a wife in a position of comfort and respect in the eyes of the community."

"And you have, Josif. You have indeed. But this is a crisis. And I'm merely helping out."

"But I worked so hard all these years!" Dr. Mustard looked both cross and confused. "I worked my fingers to the bone to give you a life of leisure, darling, where you wouldn't have to demean yourself with work."

"Josif!" Mrs. Mustard's voice became a bit sharp; Thekla was surprised. "Your mother worked *her* whole life, and work didn't demean her; it dignified her. You admired and adored her for her zeal and industry!"

"And I swore you wouldn't have to live the hard life she did!" he stormed. "Her life was an unending ordeal of backbreaking labor."

"But Josif, I don't *have* to do this," she said more softly. "I'm choosing to do it. There's nothing more to say about it. I've given my word."

"I love you, Norma Jean," Dr. Mustard said. "Isn't that enough for you?"

"What a ridiculous question," said Mrs. Mustard fondly, and Thekla could tell that her mother had won. What a surprise!

"But what are you going to teach, Mom?" she asked. "How to wash spice jars?"

"Show up in class tomorrow and find out!" said her mother, going to hang up her coat. Her tone was a bit snappy. Interesting.

"Thekla," said Dr. Mustard tiredly, "a little more respect for your mother, please."

Thekla tromped off to bed, thinking, My parents are *nuts*.

So Monday morning came around, a windless day of high clouds and glassy light. Mrs. Mustard was there to usher Miss Earth's students to their classroom.

"This is so embarrassing," muttered Thekla to no one in particular. As, alphabetically, she followed Forest Eugene Mopp into the room, she thought: In such a few days, how unlike my life my life has become. I used to be Empress of the Tattletales, the club I myself founded half a lifetime ago. Now I am a common citizen. My teacher has been abducted or swept off her feet, or she has run away for secret reasons. And now my mother, who is often too shy to go to the post office and sends me, is fiddling around in the front of my classroom looking as if she's going to break into "Getting to Know You" or "Do-Re-Mi."

"Shall we sing a little song?" said Mrs. Mustard brightly. "How about 'Getting to Know You'?"

No one wanted to be rude to a parent, but the

students could not bring themselves to reply.

Thekla raised her hand. Her mother looked at a seating chart, pretending to find out who it was. "Let's see, you must be—Thekla?" She said it *Theek*-lah instead of *Theck*-lah. The class laughed in a respectful way, though it wasn't a very funny joke.

Thekla for one was annoyed. "May I recommend taking attendance first?" she hissed.

"Oh, yes." Mrs. Mustard flustered about with the class list. Everyone was present except Thud Tweed.

Hmmm, thought Thekla. I wonder if the state troopers have taken him into custody. He had started out a bad egg, for sure. He had seemed to reform for a while, but probably he had reverted to his true nature. Which was rotten.

"Now, let's see," said Mrs. Mustard. "I'm not sure how to proceed. Tell me what you've been learning lately. I'm sure you've covered things like colors, and numbers, and basic shapes: squares, circles, triangles." She strode around the room stroking her chin. "Days of the week, seasons of the year, et cetera." She looked as if she'd like to be smoking a pipe and carrying a magnifying glass. "You know your basic alphabet, right?"

Salim Bannerjee raised his hand. With his British Empire accent (he was from Calcutta originally), he qualified as the politest-sounding student, so his message didn't seem offensive. "Mrs. Mustard. As children go, we are fairly well educated already. May I propose that we spend time working on our Science Fair projects? This way when Miss Earth comes back to us, we can surprise her by having accomplished something."

Mrs. Mustard asked to be told what the Science Fair projects were. Salim explained about the Wheel of Life. "It sounds as if Miss Earth was speaking about the food chain," said Mrs. Mustard. "The little fish is eaten by the bigger fish, who is eaten by the bigger fish, et cetera. But how are you going to work on this? Can you tell me what your topics are?"

The children did.

"I see," said Mrs. Mustard. "So. Microbes, fleas, mice, cats, dogs, wolves, bears, and people. Who would like to tell me what you've got so far?"

No one would. They hadn't gotten much yet, with all the excitement.

"Oh, don't be shy. You're making my work harder." She picked a student at random. "Pearl? Why don't you start? Your partner is absent today. What can you tell us about your research into human beings?"

"Very little," said Pearl. "I'm always too busy babysitting my six siblings to get to the library."

"Well—maybe we should think about a field trip, then."

"Yes. We need to work in the library," said Lois Kennedy the Third. "We take turns surfing the Net and we ransack the encyclopedia. Mr. Dewey gets a headache finding books and magazine articles for us. It's very rewarding. It teaches us research skills."

"Very well," said Mrs. Mustard dubiously. "Get on your coats. We'll walk to the library. Now we might as well line up according to the pairs that Miss Earth assigned you to be. Nina and Mike. Carly and Stan. Sharday and Moshe. Anna Maria and Forest Eugene. Fawn and Hector. Lois and Salim. Sammy and Thekla. And Pearl, since your partner is absent, I'll work with you. Now let's everyone hold hands with our partner—"

The entire class shrieked in protest.

"Well, scrap that suggestion," said Mrs. Mustard. "We'll just walk two by two, then. We don't have to hold hands."

"Thekla," whispered Sammy Grubb, "we have *got* to find Miss Earth."

"You're telling me," said Thekla grimly. Having your mother enjoy a new professional challenge was one thing, but having to witness it was proving quite another.

When they arrived at the library, Mr. Dewey met them at the door. "Oh, dear," he said. "This isn't really a good time."

"This isn't a good time to visit the library?" asked Mrs. Mustard. "The *public* library?"

"Well, come in," said Mr. Dewey. "But you'll have to conduct your research without my help. I'm busy for a little while."

The children saw what he meant. Behind the library were three state troopers, blocking off the muddy lawn with yellow police-barrier tape. The fellow they knew, Trooper Hiram Crawdad, was taking photographs. Nearby, Grandma Earth stood hunched in a down vest. "I have to go assist in the investigation," said Mr. Dewey. "I mean, as librarian, I am responsible for library property, which includes not just books, periodicals, videotapes, and CDs, but also the parking lot and the grass."

"Do not stand and peer out the windows," said Mrs. Mustard. "Class, to your work. Class, listen to me. *Class.*"

No one listened.

Mrs. Mustard decided teaching was harder than she'd thought. She went and looked up April Fool's Day in the encyclopedia. She learned that the word *April* probably derived from a Latin verb *aperire,* "to open." The time when bulbs open. But it might also have derived from *aper,* the Latin word for "wild boar." Now, a wild boar might just qualify as being higher on the food chain

172

than wolves, bears, and people. Even teachers.

But April Fool's Day? Its origins were uncertain. In the fourteenth century, the Western calendar was altered. January became the start of the new year instead of springtime, or April. Folks who resisted making the change were called April fools, and tricks were played on them. Could Miss Earth's disappearance be nothing but a huge April Fool's trick? wondered Mrs. Mustard.

"Hey," said someone, "Thud Tweed is with them!"

"Hi, Thud!" the students yelled. They pounded on the window and waved. If Thud heard the commotion, they couldn't tell; he didn't turn.

"They got the goods on you?" called Lois Kennedy the Third.

"He's innocent until proven guilty!" called Sammy Grubb.

"Don't arrest my research partner!" called Pearl Hotchkiss rather bravely. "I don't want to have to do all the work by myself!"

"You going to juvenile jail?" called Nina Bueno.

"Send us letters!" called Hector Yellow. "We can be pen pals!"

"We'll spring you out! We'll tunnel you out! We'll send you a nail file hidden in a burrito!" called Stan Tomaski.

"Take dance classes!" called Sharday Wren. "Learn a trade!"

"Don't get beat up by bigger kids!" called Moshe Cohn, who was the smallest boy in the class. "Remember the Circle of Life! You're a human being, not a Missing Link! Use your brains, not your brawn! Outwit your adversaries!"

"Shhhhh!" said Mrs. Mustard. "This is a library."

"Thud," called Thekla, abandoning the comical tone, "remember my grandmother's motto. Beware what you choose."

"Thud!" said Salim—who didn't even like him much. Who partly blamed Thud's Flameburper crony, Amos, for the death of his Flameburper friend, Seymour. "Thud!" said Salim, hammering against the glass. "Don't go! Run away!"

"Hey," said Moshe Cohn in a smaller voice. "Where are they taking him?"

She turned a bit. She was conscious of her parts—her eyes, her fingers, her knees. But she was paralyzed. She couldn't move. Her thinking was sluggish. Have I been buried alive? she wondered. Is that why it is so dark? Why can't I flex my arches or crack my knuckles? I can't even swallow or blink. My bladder and bowels are

still. If I'm dead, oughtn't I be moving toward a door-
way of light, to the strains of heavenly music of some
sort?

I wanted music for my wedding, she remembered.
Not for my funeral.

Oh, Tim!

18

Nobody's Business

When the class returned from the library and settled back down, they looked to Thekla's mother to see what ridiculous thing she'd do next.

But while they'd been staring out the window, Norma Jean Mustard had been talking to Mr. Dewey. On his advice she had borrowed from the library a collection of stories by a writer named Frank Stockton.

"I'm going to read aloud to you," she told them. "An exciting story called 'The Lady or the Tiger?'"

The children, raised on the fine literature Miss Earth chose, did not expect much from "The Lady or the Tiger?"

The story was written in a lush, dense style. At first it was hard to follow, but then they got into it. A barbarian king became angry when he found out that his royal daughter had been carrying on with a handsome commoner. The king threw the man into a public arena. Only two doors opened into this space. Behind one door, a ravenous tiger was waiting. Behind the other, a beautiful woman. The man had to choose which door to open, not knowing what was behind it. If the tiger emerged, the man would be eaten in a flash. If the woman emerged, the man would be married to her on the spot. But which door was which? And which should he choose?

And then when no one was looking but the hapless man, the king's daughter cunningly indicated one of the doors. But was she mad with jealousy over the thought of her boyfriend's falling into the arms of another woman? Or was she noble enough to prefer that he live happily ever after with someone else, even if she had to suffer loneliness? Was she saving him or betraying him?

Which should he choose?

And there the story ended.

"Well, which *did* he choose?" asked Sammy Grubb, who'd been listening despite himself.

"What do you think?" said Mrs. Mustard.

"I don't know!" said Sammy. "It's the author's job to tell us!"

"He didn't, this time," said Mrs. Mustard. "You have to imagine it for yourself."

"People in love can read each other's thoughts," said Carly Garfunkel. "He'd know what she was thinking."

"Maybe he'd prefer to be eaten by a tiger than have to marry anyone at all," said Mike Saint Michael. "I would."

"I hate modern fiction," said Sammy Grubb. "Give me the solid, reliable *National Enquirer* anytime."

"*Uwazaj co wybierasz,*" said Thekla Mustard. "Beware what you choose."

After school the Copycats and the Tattletales hung out together, trudging along Squished Toad Road. With Thud in some sort of custody, and Pearl as usual off to babysit, there were only the seven Copycats and the seven Tattletales. Even though the Tattletales had a new leader, it ought to have felt like business as usual, boys versus girls. This was how the school year had begun, when the Siberian snow spiders had escaped from a truck accident and overrun the Josiah Fawcett Elementary School.

That seemed so simple, so long ago! Now everything was distressing and serious. The sunlight fell down the slopes of April clouds in its usual fashion, the new grass was the color of leprechauns' waistcoats, but the world had lost its power to charm.

🦂 🦂 🦂

Arriving at Fingerpie Farm, they found Flossie mending a fence with a treacherous length of barbed wire. She had six nails in her mouth, so when Lois asked her if there was anything new with Beatrice, Flossie could only answer, "Irxtrittle penucky pirthbroo, scklommy."

Then she hammered two nails and spit out four more, and repeated herself. "She's a different creature since she hatched out of that cocoon. I don't mean what she looks like; anyone can dress up now and then. I mean she's feistier. She's less fearful. Before, she seemed terrified of the great outdoors. Now she wants to get out."

"Why don't you let her?" asked Lois Kennedy the Third. "Can't she take care of herself, equipped with that little flamethrower throat of hers?"

"Whatever's been stalking this farm is *clever*," said Flossie morosely. "I went to the back shed to get some barbed wire and found that someone had stolen a length of it from one of my reels. Farmers don't steal from each other, and barbed wire is a bit hard to steal. A bit ouchy. But it's gone as gone."

"What're you doing with that barbed wire anyway?" asked Salim. "Isn't that sort of nasty, for a farm?"

"I'll tell you what's nasty," said Flossie Fingerpie. "Some critter broke through the electrified lines of the upland pasture last night. Might have got one of my ewes if I hadn't been up with a bladder problem. I got my gun and scared it off the property—this time. But I don't want to meet it coming down for breakfast. I'll tell you that right now. *That's* why I'm doing reinforcements here. I got a right to protect my flock."

"What could it be? Coydog?"

"I'm afraid the culprit is something stronger. Bobcat, maybe. They're coming back into the north woods, big-time."

But Flossie didn't mention that she'd never heard of a bobcat that could break through barbed, electrified fence wire, snap it as if it were spiderwebs. Flossie kept her worries to herself.

They headed toward the barn. "Your friend ain't there," said Flossie. "She's too antsy to be cooped up all night and all day. She's out back in the hen yard. Not much room for her to strut, but it's better than nothing."

They circled around the barn. The hen yard was fenced with chicken wire. With her little prehensile front claws and her less useful rear ones, Beatrice was trying to teach herself to scale the fence. Hand over hand, or claw over claw—but she couldn't get the pattern of movements right, and kept falling to the ground.

"Something's gotten into her," said Sammy. "She's developing some nerve as well as some skill. What's she after?"

"Maybe whatever is after *her* got this far," said

Thekla Mustard. "Maybe she wants to engage in battle. I mean, look. If the stalker snapped the fence where Flossie's working, it could have come down through the paddock and around this way."

"If it snapped *that* fence, it could have *shredded* this one," said Hector.

"Maybe it was about to. Look. Feathers."

A flurry of brownish feathers had gotten caught among the stubbly growth around the corner fence post. They were bigger than the feathers of Beatrice's green topknot, and slightly sinister-looking, like a set of brown fletched skewers.

"Look," said Nina, "something has been working here. Maybe it was trying to dig under the fence when Mrs. Fingerpie woke up and scared it away."

The earth was disturbed with a look of clawmarks. Bits of straw and bracken, not unlike those Beatrice had used to make her cocoon, were scattered about. Other things too: a bit of masking tape here, a shred of old snakeskin, a long loop of material with a bit of embroidery worked into it . . .

"Is that . . . ?" said Lois. She peered more closely. "It certainly seems to be . . ." She tugged it loose.

It was a scrap of material with a black background, and yellow grosbeaks with uplifted beaks printed in a comical row.

It was the edge of Miss Earth's shawl. The one she'd been wearing on the afternoon when she was last seen.

"Just what is going on here?" Lois asked Beatrice sternly.

"What's up?" said Thud.

The children turned. Thud had sidled up alongside the barn. Though the afternoon light was behind him and made the children squint, he did not appear to be wearing black and white stripes, nor the chains and shackles of someone newly escaped from a minimum-security prison.

"You're back," said Sammy Grubb a bit cautiously.

"I was helping with the investigation," said Thud. "I had to tell the trooper everything—about the Copycats, and the Tattletales, and the April Fool's joke that the girls were playing on the boys. I told them how I dressed up as a gorilla and where I was waiting when Lois and the Tattletales led you gullible Copycat boys down Foggy Hollow. I showed them where I flung the gorilla mask into the water. I don't know why they wanted to know all that. I think they just don't have any other leads. But we traipsed up and down Foggy Hollow all day. We found a creepy stretch where an old spiderweb was hung between several trees—it was about nine feet across, and though the filaments were thin, they were strong as steel. They seem to have lasted all winter, even

182

bearing the weight of snow and ice. Something's amiss in Foggy Hollow, I do believe, but it isn't a Missing Link and it isn't me."

"That's where the Siberian snow spiders made their home!" said Sammy Grubb. "I hope you didn't see any spider sacs hanging nearby, waiting to erupt with thousands of infant snow spiders."

"I didn't," said Thud.

"What was Trooper Crawdad looking for?" asked Sammy.

"He had one of Mayor Grass's work boots," said Thud. "He was looking for a bootprint that matched. Mayor Grass has no alibi for a week ago today. He says he was home sleeping, but he lives alone, and no one can verify it. So he's still under suspicion."

"Is he in custody?"

"They don't have a motive or any clues. They can't pin a thing on him yet, far as I can tell."

"The mood is still mean in town, though," said Sammy. "Mayor Grass isn't someone it's easy to mistrust. But without any other suspects, he's in a vulnerable position."

"Thanks to Thekla," said Lois. "She's the one who fingered him."

"All I did was mention a little tiff I witnessed," said Thekla. "I never said Mayor Grass was a criminal of any sort. I just said he might have a motive."

"Well, half the town agrees with you," said Lois. "Even I think it's smart to be cautious about him."

"Look," said Thekla, "until we find out what happened, and who if anybody is responsible, it's reasonable to wonder about anyone."

"Any of us could have a *motive*," said Thud. "I mean, she was our teacher."

"*Is* our teacher!" several children anxiously corrected him.

"You know what I mean. Kids take against their teachers from time to time. Once when I was at the Aaron Burr Military Academy for Boys, some guys and I took against this drill sergeant, see, and we—"

"*I don't want to know,*" said Thekla. "Thud, don't be ridiculous. We all love Miss Earth to death."

Everyone looked at her. "Well, maybe I should rephrase that," she said.

"Look," said Sammy, "if we can't do much to find Miss Earth, we should at least try to remove suspicion from Mayor Grass."

"But we need a culprit, a motive, and a clue," said Thud. "We need something."

Lois said, "Good news, Thud. We have no culprit and we have even less motive. But we have a clue." She held up the scrap of material. "This was torn from the shawl Miss Earth was wearing the day she disappeared. We just found it here, caught in the webbing of chicken wire, where someone or something was trying to get at Beatrice the Flameburper last night."

"Someone?" said Thud. "Like who? That scientist from Massachusetts who was hunting for her a month ago? We put him way off the trail, didn't we? Or you said some*thing*? Like what? You mean like a fox? A bear? A raccoon? Something else?"

"Hey, kids," Flossie Fingerpie yelled from the fence. "You know, with all the commotion, I think I've misplaced Doozy. Do you see her back there?"

Doozy? Doozy Dorking? "No," said Thekla. "When did you see her last?"

"This morning, surely. Or was that yesterday morning?" muttered Flossie. "Oh, cripes, did something get her?"

"Doozy!" called Lois, and the others took up the call. "Doozy!"

They ducked out of the barn. No sign, no dim distracted cluck.

"Hey, what if the stalker got Doozy?" said Lois. "You know she has a habit of fluttering up to a post when she gets nervous. Maybe she fluttered up—and something got her."

"Doozy's always seemed a bit slow, I'll admit,"

bawled Flossie. "But I doubt she'd throw herself into harm's way out of sheer forgetfulness. The survival instinct is stronger than that."

"Still," said Lois. They looked at Beatrice. "Maybe that's what's gotten into her. She's trying to rescue her stepchicken."

Thud marched over to the gate. He lifted his foot like a professional soccer player, and with one swift motion he unhooked the gate and flung it open.

Beatrice scurried through in a flash.

"Hey!" shouted Lois. "What are you doing?" She and the rest of the class didn't wait to hear the answer. They raced after Beatrice.

Thud didn't have words to explain his actions anyway. They all made a sort of mixed-up fizz inside of him. It was something about *release from prison* and *rescue your mother* and *freak on the loose*. But mostly his thought was the same as everyone else's:

Follow that Flameburper!

So he did.

19

Missing, Presumed Dead

She was aware of a little bit more, but only in swift and fleeting perceptions. She couldn't even tell if she was thinking the same thing over and over every time she struggled into a vague state of half waking, or if she was claiming new thoughts.

She could tell there was something spiky wrapped around her. Thorny brambles, maybe, or barbed wire. She couldn't even see them, but when an involuntary twitch of electrochemical energy made one of her muscles spasm, she could feel thorns spear her skin.

She felt them, she knew what they were, but they didn't hurt. Maybe she had been anesthetized.

She struggled to remember her life. It was hard. But her mouth remembered thirst. When moisture seeped through the impenetrably black matting of her prison, her mouth remembered to open. Though she couldn't even swallow, much less cry out for help, she could hold her throat open long enough for water to trickle down.

Once she hiccuped. Once, and only once. But by that hiccup she became fairly sure that she was still alive. The dead don't hiccup.

The Tattletales and the Copycats and Thud Tweed hurried around the corner of the barn. "She went thataway," Flossie Fingerpie said and pointed toward the road. "How'd she get out? And what's gotten into that little bundle of bravado? You'd better catch her before she gets run over by some speeding maniac from Massachusetts or New York."

Beatrice made pretty good time along Squished Toad Road, heading southeast toward the village. The kids hurried at a mid-speed ramble, half jogging, half walking. It was embarrassing to be chasing a freak of nature, but this was Vermont, and freaks of nature have rights too, including the right not to be run over by a visitor doing sixty in a forty-mile-an-hour zone.

Beatrice looked for all the world like a dog following a scent. She careered back and forth across the road, disappearing into gulleys made muddy by spring runoff, appearing again. She'd pause, sniff, listen, scratch, lift her scaly neck, backtrack, and then set off again. Her movements were swift and jerky, but her progress was mercifully slow. With effort the children were able to keep pace with her.

By the time Beatrice scurried into town, the trail she was following must have become compromised by other sensory information. She slowed down and seemed unsure, turning this way, that. When she got to the Hamlet Free Community Library, she ducked through a broken lattice underneath the porch and paused there as if to review her options.

Mrs. Mustard was just leaving the library with a stack of books. "Thank you, Mr. Dewey," she was saying. "You've been a big help. Good heavens," she continued at the sight of the Tattletales, the Copycats, and Thud. "The library's popular today. Are you children all here to do research on your Science Fair projects?"

"Beatrice the Flameburper is underneath the front porch, Mom," said Thekla.

"She wants to use the library?" Mr. Dewey looked down over the tops of his half-glasses. "She's welcome, of course, as long as she keeps her mouth shut and doesn't engage in book burning. We don't believe in censorship here."

Beatrice stuck her head out and sniffed the air again.

"She's a lot like a crocodile, isn't she?" said Mrs. Mustard. "A crocodile with useless little wings."

Irritated, Beatrice blew a puff of smoke, like a teenage delinquent on a street corner. She used her wings to fan the puff of smoke up into Mrs. Mustard's face. "Pee-yew," said Mrs. Mustard, making a face. "Foul."

"Don't bring *that* up," groaned Sammy Grubb.

"Her feet seem much smaller than those footprints in the concrete of the school's new sidewalk," said Mrs. Mustard. "I was looking at those prints during lunch break today, wondering who made them. They looked reptilian to me, so I've been doing research with Mr. Dewey's help. Do you know what we learned about crocodiles?"

"No," said Sammy warily, trying to edge toward Beatrice to snatch her.

"The word itself is interesting—it's from the Greek *kroke* plus *drilos*—pebble worm. See how leathery Beatrice's skin is? It would be well camouflaged at the bottom of a river, a pebbly river. You could walk on it and never even know the difference. Until the river bottom opened up its jaws and took off your foot, of course."

"Nice," said Thekla, angling to grab Beatrice from the other direction.

"Isn't education interesting?" said Mrs. Mustard. "I'm quite enjoying myself. See you at home, dear." She left.

Mr. Dewey said, "I was about to shut down the computers and turn out the lights. You kids need any emergency reading material?"

Nobody did just now. They were all too busy arranging themselves in a human net around the library porch, to snare a Flameburper.

"Bye, then." Mr. Dewey returned to the library.

Beatrice took a couple of big breaths, as if getting ready to make a run for it.

"Who made that footprint in the concrete, by the way?" Thekla muttered to Lois. "Who did you assign to do that job?"

"I didn't assign anyone," said Lois. "I assumed one of us was taking initiative, something Tattletales rarely did under *your* leadership, Thekla." She glanced aside at the other Tattletales. "So who had that bright idea, by the way? I thought maybe it was you, Carly."

"It wasn't me," said Carly.

"Not me," echoed Sharday, Anna Maria, and Nina, one by one.

"What bright idea?" said Fawn, who had forgotten the question.

"Did one of you do it?" asked Thekla of Sammy Grubb and the boys.

"Are you nuts? I mean even more than usual?" replied Sammy. "That Missing Link trick was *on* us, not *by* us. It must have been Thud."

"Don't tar me with that brush," said Thud. "I've done a fair amount of vandalism of school property in my day, but I haven't lifted a finger to mess up a wall or a window or a newly poured sidewalk in Vermont. Believe me. I'm in a confessional mood these days. If I had done it, I'd admit it."

"Could Mayor Grass have done it?" said Thekla. "He helped pour the cement, after all. Maybe he came back and stamped it with a phony footprint, to throw the authorities off his trail."

"That was the week before. There was no trail to throw people off," Lois pointed out. "Miss Earth hadn't disappeared yet."

Thud said, "I think your mother is right, Thekla. From what I remember of it, that print *did* look sort of reptilian."

"We don't have any large reptiles in Vermont," said Forest Eugene Mopp—known as Mr. Science from time to time. "To my knowledge."

"They say there are crocodiles in the sewers of New York," Thud reminded them. "Maybe one escaped and moved to the country."

"I know what you're all doing, and it *won't work*," said Sammy. "It's really mean of you to try to trick me again into thinking there's something else out there."

He glowered at his friends. Beatrice took this chance to try to escape again. She lunged out from under the porch into a muddy patch. Sammy lunged at her in desperation, even rage; she paused, flicking her head this way and that, and then ducked away.

She left a footprint in the mud. It was just like the footprint immortalized in the cement of the new school pavement.

Only way, way smaller. It gave Sammy a funny thrill. . . .

"Compadres," said Thud Tweed, "if none of us made a decoy footprint as part of an April Fool's joke, then something else did. Something capable of attacking Forest Eugene's dog and worrying a Fingerpie sheep and Lord knows what else. Maybe something capable of attacking Miss Earth. Kids," he continued, "all our silly jokes about the Missing Link aside, there is something *still out there.*"

"There she goes!" shouted Thekla. "Into Foggy Hollow."

20

The Eureka Moment

By now the children were weary. Hector had a charley horse. Sharday was worried about putting runs in her tights. But Lois said, "Beatrice is going somewhere. This is like an old episode of *Lassie*."

"Lassie never had a stepmother who was a chicken!" protested Thud, who had spent more hours in front of TV reruns than most people, and knew his stuff.

"Maybe Beatrice means for us to follow," said Lois. "Look how she pauses to make sure we're still here."

"If there's something in this overgrowth," said Stan, "it'll sure hear us. We sound like a herd of elephants."

"Safety in numbers," said Thekla. "Everybody, stay close."

"Who wants to get close to *you*?" said Thud. "Be real."

No one laughed. They were all too tired. Luckily, Beatrice was slowing down. This gave the kids a chance to catch up a little.

Then they arrived at the web that Thud had reported finding, the web spun by Siberian snow spiders six months earlier. It was half as broad as a badminton net, and twice as tall, and it hung like a pirate's flag of doom in the fading afternoon light. For a moment, Thekla thought that it had been woven out of the barbed wire stolen from Fingerpie Farm. Then she saw that the web trailed scraps of filament, and that the corpses of bugs and field mice were wound tight and wrapped with cord, hanging like horrible ornaments off the swaying fretwork.

"Those poor dead creatures," said Sammy Grubb. "The spiders did some careful packaging, didn't they, to preserve their meals? Those shrouds look a lot like the cocoon Beatrice emerged from. . . ." Again, Sammy felt a shiver of foreboding.

"Beatrice?" called Lois. "Where *did* you go?"

While the children had stood staring at the web, the Flameburper had vanished.

"We could separate into two groups—Tattletales and Copycats—and look in two different directions," said Lois Kennedy the Third.

"Oh, well," said Thud, "we could also pair off with

our Science Fair partners and hold hands like Mrs. Mustard suggested, and we could wander about like lovebirds in the dusk." He grinned, because his Science Fair partner, Pearl, wasn't there to have to hold hands with.

"Nothing doing," said Thekla Mustard. "I'm not holding hands with Sammy Grubb for love or money, even if my mother orders me to."

They stood for a moment, irresolute. At this hour the woods had a murky aspect. You could almost feel the woods thinking: Go ahead, wait. The longer you wait, the darker it'll get.

"You all can do what you like," Sharday Wren declared at last. "This place is a mite too creepy for me. Friends, I am outta here."

"Me too," said Carly and Anna Maria. "Let's go."

Hector and Forest Eugene and Stan looked a bit miserable, as if they'd have liked to admit their own timidity but were too timid to.

"But what about Beatrice!" said Lois.

"It's your baby Flameburper lost in these woods," said Thud. "As you keep pointing out. So if you want her, go after her yourself."

Sammy Grubb said, "Look, everyone. Either we all stick together here, or we all leave."

So everyone sighed theatrically and shrugged as if

there were nothing to be done but, well, *leave*. And the faster the better.

And they did, hauling themselves back up the slope to the edge of Ethantown Road.

Preparing to squirm at her father's nosey questions about her mother in the classroom that day, Thekla turned south with Carly Garfunkel and Forest Eugene Mopp, who lived on Chumptown Road. The other children headed back toward the green, there to spread out and make their plodding ways home. Thud got ready to tell Grandma Earth how the state troopers had conducted their investigation on this, the seventh day of her daughter's absence. Lois knew she had to stop by Fingerpie Farm and report to Flossie Fingerpie that Beatrice had disappeared in Foggy Hollow.

And Sammy Grubb got home and saw a note from his mom on the table:

Feeling lucky tonite! Dad and I out to Bingo at St. Anselm's in Forbush Corners. Supper in the microwave. Don't forget homework!

Hmmmm, thought Sammy Grubb.

Then he went out to the old Chevy sitting on cinder blocks in the side yard. Mr. Grubb kept his tools locked in its trunk. Sammy found the industrial-strength flashlight with its heavy battery and tested it. The juice was good; light stung the lawn into an unnatural evening greenness. The thing was too heavy and bulky to carry in one hand, so Sammy Grubb went inside to grab his school backpack. He packed up the flashlight and went to the phone.

Mayor Grass answered after two rings.

"Any news about Miss Earth?" asked Sammy.

"Look, Sammy," said Mayor Grass, "don't you worry yourself about this. Let the grownups take care of grown-up problems."

"People are getting ugly," said Sammy Grubb.

"I'm not alarmed," said Mayor Grass. But Sammy Grubb thought his voice sounded careful—maybe quietly alarmed. "People know who I am. They're just worried, and I can't blame them. But the best minds in Vermont law enforcement are on the case. So relax."

Sammy Grubb wasn't much consoled by Trooper Hiram Crawdad's being the best mind in Vermont law enforcement.

He hung up the phone. Missing Link or missing teacher or missing Flameburper or missing hen, Sammy was not about to miss this opportunity to find something. Anything. Whether his classmates wanted to join him or not.

🐒 🐒 🐒

It was slow going in Foggy Hollow. Directly above Sammy—he could see it because most of the trees down here were still in the early stages of budding and had not yet blotted out the view with leaves—the sky was like inky smoke. On either side of him, though, thanks to the steep slopes of the ravine, night had come early and thoroughly.

Sammy Grubb felt as far away from civilization as it was possible to feel in central Vermont.

Not knowing precisely what he was looking for, he swung the light slowly from side to side, illuminating the path ahead, the edges of the mucky stream. Amazing how many things glint at night in the woods.

Beatrice might have given up on finding Doozy—assuming that had been her goal. She might have retraced her steps. Right now she might be enjoying a well-earned supper of seed corn and bugs and mash back at Fingerpie Farm. But Sammy Grubb had the sense that Lois was right. Lois was a kind of co-stepmother, with Doozy Dorking, of Beatrice. Lois had an instinct that Beatrice was on to something, though what—what—Sammy could not imagine.

He peered, he pushed forward, he peered again, he listened. Once, his foot sank into the stream wriggling its way along the bottom of Foggy Hollow. His sock filled up with icy water, and he said a bad word that he never would have said in front of anyone. He said it again when his foot slipped and he knelt, suddenly, in the water, and the cold ran its greasy grip along his calves and halfway up his thigh. Now he'd be chilled, and he'd have to turn back before long. Drat double drat!

He pulled the flashlight out of the water, and quickly he tried to wring the excess liquid out of his jeans. He had slipped because the rocks of the old streambed, newly wet again, were slick, even slimy. Like the back of a lizard, he thought, like that crocodile—pebbly worm—that Mrs. Mustard had been talking about.

Then the flashlight battery went dead and Sammy was plunged into darkness. But at the same time another light went on—the light in his brain—and Sammy thought: Eureka. Eureka! I have found it!

He didn't know exactly what had happened to Miss Earth. He couldn't put all the pieces together at once. But whatever it was that had happened, Sammy Grubb had a pretty good hunch who was responsible.

21

Triple Whammy?

When Sammy Grubb got back to his house, his parents still weren't home. But the phone rang while he was trying to think what to do, and Sammy was pleased that it was his mom. "We're on a roll, sweetheart," she said. "We won sixty-five bucks in the first few games! Did you eat yet?"

"Mom," said Sammy, "I have a theory about what happened to Miss Earth."

"Honey, I can't hear you—they're hooting and hollering here," said Mrs. Grubb. "Come again?"

Sammy explained his notions. Mrs. Grubb said, "Well now, Sammy, that's pretty far-fetched. But you've got a good head on your shoulders like your daddy, and you should follow your instincts. If we could get home right away, I'd say wait for us, but our truck is blocked by other vehicles. It'll take a while to sort all that out. What I'd do if I were you is call Mayor Grass."

"Even though he's been under suspicion of foul play?" said Sammy.

"You and I both know that's a lot of hooey," said his mom. "Just call him. And call Grandma Earth, for goodness' sakes. She's wasting away with worry. Any new theory, even an oddball one like yours, has got to be better than nothing, doesn't it?"

"I guess so," said Sammy. "Bye. And good luck."

"We'll be back as soon as we can," said his mom.

Mayor Grass didn't answer his phone this time.

It was darker than dark now. Sammy didn't want to go back into Foggy Hollow without Mayor Grass and another witness—someone who could testify, if need be, that Timothy Grass had nothing to do with whatever was found there. Sammy didn't know whether waiting another few hours might put Miss Earth at greater risk, but he didn't want to put Mayor Grass at risk either. In the end, he decided to sit on the sofa until his parents got home. And there he fell asleep, and when they got home, his parents covered him with a blanket. They let him snooze on the sofa while they took themselves to bed.

Sammy had a dream, an ordinary dream. It wasn't

about Missing Links or Abominable Snowmen or Snow-women. It wasn't about Loch Ness monsters or space aliens or killer anchovies invading Manhattan or Montpelier.

It was about Sleeping Beauty, of all things. Only the Sleeping Beauty was Miss Earth, and she wasn't in a tower behind a thorny bramble. She was wrapped in the thorny bramble herself, like the human stuffing inside a very nonvegetarian burrito.

Sammy didn't want to hack her out and save her. That was Mayor Tim Grass's job. Sammy just wanted to make sure Mayor Grass got there in time.

And when the first pearl-beige light began to temper the blackness of night with the character of dawn, Sammy woke up. He could tell by the blanket that his parents were home. He knew it was too early to call anyone. He dialed Mayor Grass anyway.

Mayor Grass listened and groggily replied, "That's pretty wild, Sammy. You have a hunch constructed out of feeble scientific theories and the memory of a fairy tale. A hunch like that is not much to go on."

"I tried to call you again later last night and you weren't in," said Sammy.

"I had driven over to Dartmouth," said Mayor Grass. "I was trying to find a tenor to hire to sing at a wedding. It was the only thing I could think of to do. Germaine—

I mean Miss Earth—had hoped to have a tenor soloist, and it consoled me to keep trying to find one."

Dimly Sammy remembered something about a tenor being part of the conversation Thekla had overheard. Was that all it was about? A discussion about who was going to sing at the wedding? If so, Thekla had been *way* out in left field.

Mayor Grass yawned. "Look, I'll meet you at the library. But as I'm still vaguely under suspicion, I think you'd better come with your parents. You want to wait until they wake up?"

"I'll meet you in half an hour," said Sammy. "With an adult, one way or another. Promise."

Then Sammy listened to the dial tone for a while and tried to compose his thoughts.

A sleepy Thud answered Grandma Earth's phone.

"Hey, it's me," said Sammy. "Sammy."

"If you're becoming a telemarketer, this isn't a good time to start," said Thud.

"I have to tell you something," said Sammy. "I have to apologize."

"Mmmm?" Thud wasn't used to receiving apologies, much less giving them, so he didn't know what to say. "You have to apologize, I have to take a pee. Who should go first?"

"Listen," said Sammy. "You asked me to trust you

and I didn't. I had good reason not to—you must admit—but I ought to have let you have one more try. I'm sorry. Anyone can change. Even people who haven't been trustworthy can change."

"Is this a late-developing April Fool's joke?" asked Thud warily. "Maybe I deserve it, Sammy, but I'm a bit sleepy to follow this."

"I mean," said Sammy, "I think I know what's in Foggy Hollow. And I even have a guess why. But I think we should ask Grandma Earth to join us. Is she up baking bread yet?"

"I think she's actually sawing Zs, for once," he said. "Do you want me to wake her?"

"I think you'd better," said Sammy.

Thud went and tiptoed to the door of Grandma Earth's room. He could see her lying on top of her covers. She'd fallen asleep in her work jeans and socks, her only concession to bedtime being the removal of her false teeth to a glass of water on her bedside table. In the dim light from the hall landing, her face looked sunken and old, almost as if she were ready to fall into a permanent rest. "Not yet," whispered Thud. "Your daughter needs you still."

In a louder voice he said, "Grandma Earth. Wake up."

"Is it the Judgment Day?" mumbled Grandma

Earth, sitting bolt upright and grabbing her teeth.

"Maybe," said Thud.

The sky had lightened to the color of bacon fat by the time Mayor Grass, Thud Tweed, Grandma Earth, and Sammy Grubb gathered on the sloping lawn behind the library. Mayor Grass and Grandma Earth had parked their pickups at opposing angles and put on their high beams, to send rivers of light in two directions down Foggy Hollow.

"Run through your theory again," said Grandma Earth. "I'm slowing down, and it takes me a while to process."

Sammy found it hard to speak deliberately. "You see, *something* made that footprint in the pavement at school, but it wasn't Beatrice. She's not big enough. And something has been scaring the Fingerpies' sheep and attacking Forest Eugene's dog and so on. We've watched how Beatrice grew—changed—developed in the past week or so. She's really gone from being a chicken to a lizard, in a way, a funny kind of lizard with wings and spontaneously combustible breath. And a crocodile is a lizard of sorts. And a crocodile, with its scaly pebbly skin, can stay underwater for a long time without coming up for breath, or appearing to."

"And you think it's Amos?" asked Mayor Grass. "The

missing Flameburper? The one who escaped?"

"Amos," said Thud. He was beset with a conflict of emotions, both worry and elation, for—to the extent a creature of the wild can manage—Amos had been *his* pet. "I get it. You think that Trooper Crawdad's colleagues and all the Hamlet residents, out searching for Miss Earth, missed Amos because he was hiding underwater."

"He was submerged in the rising stream from the week's strong rains, I bet," said Sammy.

"How could Amos have gotten bigger than Beatrice in the same amount of time?" asked Grandma Earth. "Big enough to attack Migraine?"

"Maybe Migraine attacked Amos first. Dogs do that sometimes," said Thud. "Maybe Amos struck back in self-defense."

"Besides," said Sammy, "every creature grows at its own rate. Miss Earth is always saying that to us kids. She says some kids reach adolescence sooner than others."

"Right, and some who finally get there decide never to leave it," muttered Grandma Earth.

"Thanks," said Thud.

"I wasn't talking about you," said Grandma Earth. "You're actually straightening out rather nicely, to my unprofessional eye."

It was good that the light was still fairly low, so Thud

could blush without anyone noticing too much.

"And remember," Sammy continued, "these Flameburpers were genetically altered to begin with, and possibly jolted by the electricity of a lightning bolt to boot. Who knows how they differ from any other creatures on the planet, and from each other?"

"Maybe Amos had a better diet than Beatrice too," said Thud. "A little bit less corn and bugs, a little bit more—meat and potatoes, so to speak."

"There is a strange kind of logic to all this," said Mayor Grass. "But I still wonder why Germaine would have come hunting for Amos."

"Somehow she got the note that Thud meant for me. Maybe she thought it was from you, Mayor Grass. Being lovey-dovey. So out she came. And I bet she just accidentally ran into Amos the Flameburper."

"We'd had a tiny difference of opinion," said Mayor Grass. "The week before. About finding a singer for the wedding. She wanted a soloist, while I preferred the Upper Valley Barbershop Quartet. But she could have anyone she wanted, anyone," he added. "I told her that. I tried to find a tenor for her myself."

"Time enough for all that," said Grandma Earth testily. "You'll be hiring the Upper Valley Barbershop Quartet to sing at her funeral if we're too late. Now let's concentrate on the search."

"You're either a genius, Sammy, or you should start writing for those science fiction shows on cable that don't make any sense," said Mayor Grass.

Sammy said, "Whoever was sniffing around the chicken run left a scrap of Miss Earth's scarf. Maybe it had gotten caught on Amos's rack of feathers. Those racks are turning spiky. That's what made me think Amos and Miss Earth both might be here."

"Well, forward, friends," said Mayor Grass. "But one other thing. Why would Amos have kidnapped Doozy?"

"Maybe to lure Beatrice here. To lure us here," said Sammy.

"Or maybe Doozy went of her own free will," said Thud. "After all, she was the stepchicken for Amos too, not just Beatrice."

"We may never know," said Grandma Earth. "Freakoid creatures are almost as mysterious as preteens. But let's not stand here and hypothesize."

Into the woods they made their way.

Dawn light bled slowly through the mist as they whacked away at creepers and hoops of shrubbery, at old browned vines sporting a salad of new growth. Time seemed to stand still.

At last they came to a huge boulder the size of a moving van. Most of it was sunk into the soil, but they could tell by the patterns of dried debris that the floodwaters of the raging stream had retreated down its shallow flanks. On the top of it, broadcasting an irritated greeting, sat Beatrice the Flameburper. She opened and closed the fan on top of her head with a dignified click, like a Chinese grandmother at a wedding reception.

Next to her, pecking at morning bugs, was Doozy Dorking, looking a bit sleep deprived but otherwise in perfectly fine health and good spirits.

And behind them—

"Eureka," said Sammy Grubb. "If I do say so myself."

"They look like rolled-up carpets," said Mayor Grass.

"They look a bit too much like shrouds," murmured Grandma Earth.

"They're cocoons," said Sammy. "Sort of like the ones the spiders made. And like the one that Beatrice emerged from, when she decided to convert to being a lizard."

"Only," added Thud, "these are about a hundred times bigger."

"You *could* fit a human being into one of those," said Mayor Grass.

There was a deadly moment of silence.

"Now, *why* are there two of them?" asked Grandma Earth. "Remind me."

Mayor Grass, Grandma Earth, and Thud stayed behind while Sammy ran to wake his parents and have them call Trooper Crawdad.

By the time the sun was high enough in the sky to burn off the morning mist, a good-sized crowd had assembled along the steep banks of both sides of the ravine at the bottom of Foggy Hollow.

The day was bright and dry, and there was a hint of warmth in the air, even in Foggy Hollow. The ferns unfolded their heads, the buds rustled, and folks kept their voices down and their eyes open as they considered the possibilities.

For better or for worse, more out of habit than anything else, Miss Earth's students gathered in their usual clusters. They didn't know if they were attending a funeral in the making or what. Sammy Grubb hurriedly told his followers about his eureka moment. The Copycats congratulated him but wished, in a way, that he'd been wrong. Look at the mess standing before them!

The Tattletales convened too. Lois Kennedy the Third was feeling chilled and frightened—and chastened. If she

211

hadn't urged her Tattletales into the next campaign in the humiliation of the Copycats, maybe none of this would have happened. She was ready to make amends, to do penance, anything, if it would appease the fates and return Miss Earth to them. "In the spirit of Miss Earth, whom we hope to rescue soon," she said, "as Empress of the Tattletales, I propose a shift in Tattletale policy. I propose that from now on, the Empress-ship be a rotating position. Once a month it can change, and we all shall take a turn."

"Even me?" said Fawn Petros.

"Even you," said Lois largely.

"Are we going to vote on this?" asked Anna Maria Mastrangelo.

"We don't need to," said Lois. "I am issuing an edict. As Empress I proclaim it, so it is. To prove I'm not going to change my mind, I will even relinquish my position today. Who would like to be Empress next?"

"I will," said Thekla Mustard. "We need someone with experience. Anyone opposed?"

No one was opposed. Lois Kennedy the Third shrugged and said, "Well, Thekla, I guess you can go back to being Empress. *Temporarily.* Won't Miss Earth be delighted when she hears we've changed our ways!"

"Thrilled," said Thekla. "Thank you, everyone.

Now, as your once and future Empress, my first act is this: I issue an edict revoking the idea of a mandatory revolving Empress-ship. I proclaim myself Empress for the rest of the school year."

"I object!" said Lois.

"Overruled," said Thekla. "Boy, power feels good again. It sits on one like an old sweater, well worn and comfy."

But Thekla's sentiments were a little false. In truth, she had her own pangs of conscience. She knew that it was her worrywarting about Mayor Grass that had cast suspicion on him. She'd have to find a way to make it up to him.

Before Lois could protest further, Trooper Crawdad began to speak through a bullhorn. "Folks! Now listen here! I've got to ask you to keep your distance! Please! I requested from Central Supply one of these here heat-sensing monitors. I'm going to try to get a reading off these big enchiladas and see if one of them has a live creature inside. If you get in the way of my scanner, you'll throw my reading off, and then where'll we be? So I'm asking you—watch out!"

The townspeople obliged, and the low murmur grew lower, then stopped altogether as Trooper Crawdad readied his equipment and went to work. Even the spring birds held their breath. Or it seemed as if they did.

"Have I got this right?" murmured Trooper Crawdad, checking the manual. "Okay. That's my baby. Now we're cooking with gas." He took aim, and everyone held their ears as if a thunderous boom would result.

Just silence. Then he pulled back and looked at what was registered on the screen, did it over for good measure, and shook his head.

"Oooh," he said, "we got trouble. They're both very much alive."

Grandma Earth swooned. She had never swooned in her life and didn't know how to do it gracefully; she just sat on the ground in an ungainly sort of squat and made an *ooooooph*ing sound as she did.

"If Germaine Earth is in one of these," said Trooper Crawdad in a stage whisper, "she's alive. Don't know what kind of state she'd be in, after a week—but she's still giving off body heat."

"But which one is she in?" said Dr. Mustard, peering through his pince-nez.

"And what's in the other?" asked Fawn Petros, who hadn't been following, quite.

"The other one is likely to be a Flameburper as big as a Kawasaki 8000 Silver Eagle," said Lois Kennedy the Third.

"Or something else," said Thud.

Everybody looked at him.

"If this Flameburper—my little Amos—could leave a claw print like Beatrice's, then he has already *been* a lizard-y crocodile-y thing for a while," said Thud. "Maybe he built himself a cocoon because he's about to turn into something else. Some third thing."

"We can't let him hatch—he'll be gargantuan!" said Widow Wendell. "A Flameburper the size of a gas pump? Monstrous—and dangerous."

"Mark my words," said Clem Fawcett. "We should burn the cocoon before he has a chance to hatch again."

"Get a torch," shouted Hank McManus.

"He's a monster! He'll eat us alive! Like he did Miss Earth!" screamed Fawn Petros.

"She's not eaten," said Mayor Grass. "She's in there. She's being held for—for a snack later on, or something."

Thud said, "Maybe she was wrapped up tight for protection from the cold—for healing."

"For whatever reason, she's in one of those," said Mayor Grass.

"But which one?"

"We don't know," said Mayor Grass. "That's why we can't burn either of them."

"Move aside!" bawled Mrs. Cobble. "School secretary

215

coming through!" She pushed her way forward. But when she got to the front of the crowd, she stopped too. All her years of experience at crisis management had not prepared her for a dilemma like this one.

"Stop, Mrs. Cobble," said Nurse Crisp. "Your endocrine is working overtime and giving you delusions of power. Take deep breaths."

"Mayor Grass," said Thekla, "I owe you an apology. I thought you might have done Miss Earth harm. I thought so because I overheard you talking one day, and you sounded sad. You were asking Miss Earth not to leave you."

"I wanted her to stick around and enjoy the sunset," said Mayor Grass. "I also wanted to work out who was going to sing for our wedding."

"If it's a solo singer you want, how about Petunia Whiner?" said Thekla.

"Good idea," said Mayor Grass, "but first things first."

"That's called a eureka moment," said Thekla. "I thought that up just now. I'm good, aren't I?"

"You're a royal pain in the neck," said Mayor Grass. "Stop talking. Now look. If we open the wrong cocoon, we run the risk of setting loose Amos the Flameburper, or whoever he's evolved into now. If he still has the power to breathe flame the way his sister does, he might set his nest on fire. We'd better be ready to roll the cocoons away from each other in case one goes up in flames."

The crowd paused. It was hard to know what to do.

"How to choose?" said Principal Buttle. "It's like Portia's suitors and the three caskets in *The Merchant of Venice*."

"It's like Pandora's box, more like," said Ms. Frazzle.

"It's like Bluebeard's chamber," said Nurse Pinky Crisp. "What'll we find in there?"

"It's like 'The Lady or the Tiger?'" said Norma Jean Mustard. "Think about it."

And it was like "The Lady or the Tiger?" That was exactly it. Two huge rolls of nestlike material—each one wrapped round, they saw in the strengthening light, with scraps of barbed wire stolen from Fingerpie Farm, with shreds and tatters of Miss Earth's shawl, with a felted matting of decayed vegetable material poked in among the ribs and struts formed by branches and tree limbs. On top of the leftmost one sat Beatrice. On top of the right one perched Doozy Dorking.

Had Beatrice done a good deed? Had she tried to lead the children to the cocoons? Had she hoped they might rescue Miss Earth, and so was she perched on

Miss Earth's cocoon? Or was Beatrice trying to indicate that she had located the cocoon of her only living sibling, Amos the Flameburper?

Or was all this a bunch of hooey? How could a mere creature *intend* to do that much good?

"While we dither," said Grandma Earth, "Germaine could be losing the function of her vital organs. Let's get to it. We can't let her suffocate because we're indecisive."

"Beware what you choose!" muttered Dr. Mustard. *"Uwazaj co wybierasz!"*

"Yes," said his wife, taking his hand, "beware, beware, but, dear Josif, we still have to choose. We can't refuse to choose just because we're scared of the possibilities."

He looked over the top of his glasses at her. "My dear Norma Jean," he said, "you have become a teacher not just of children, but also of me. I do believe you're right. We must choose, and live with our choices."

In a smaller voice, so as not to embarrass her in front of her students, he added, "And I choose you, my dear; again and again and again." And he held her hand.

Doozy Dorking squawked. Beatrice looked at her with a teenager's disgust and embarrassment at being yelled at in public. But she scrambled down the cocoon she was sitting on and went to join her stepchicken on the other one.

Then Doozy squawked again and nestled into the matted matter as if nothing would move her for some time, and she wanted to see a show.

"Okay, Doozy," said Mayor Grass. "Maybe you know best."

"Or maybe it's a triple whammy," muttered Thud, "and we get the big fire-breathing Missing Link that Sammy's been hankering after. . . ."

Mayor Grass went forward and thrust his hands into the matted straw and mud of the cocoon Beatrice had just abandoned. "Eeny, meeny, miney, moe. One two three and away we go." He began to pull material away.

The whole town of Hamlet was in a state of shock, a state of quiet alarm, immobilized, like statues, like a tableau, like those in the arena at the end of the story, waiting to see what came out of the door.

It was morning. It was a dream of sunlight. Miss Earth knew several things. She remembered her name was Miss Earth. She remembered what light looked like— how it hurt the eyes with its sharp brightness. She found herself blinking. She didn't know if her spirit was finally being released from her body, and she was drifting, floating toward the eternal light of heaven, or if this was the old ordinary poky sunlight of springtime in Vermont. She almost didn't care. Light was light. It was all good. She blinked again. Can the dead blink? Tears stood in her eyes.

22

April Showers
Bring May Flowers

By the time Miss Earth's head was unwrapped from the cocoon, feeling had begun to come back into her extremities. Having been numb for a week, she would have a powerful urge to use the bathroom in a short while.

Everyone joined in to tear the rest of the cocoon to shreds. How densely packed the handwoven stuffing was! It must have taken long hours of work to knit.

"We have no proof that Amos the Flameburper ever intended Germaine harm," said Mayor Grass, when his tears of relief had slowed down some. "Perhaps Thud is right. Did you fall on a slippery patch and brain yourself, my darling? Did Amos save you, wrap you up tight to keep you safe and warm?"

Miss Earth couldn't nod yes or shake her head no.

They'd have to wait to learn the truth. Assuming she would make a full recovery . . .

"We have no proof he *wasn't* intending her for a snack when he got good and hungry, either," said Clem Fawcett.

"True," said Mayor Grass. "But we have a choice in how we look at things. Until we know for sure, we should give Amos the benefit of the doubt."

"The same as we ought to have given you, I suppose," said Clem. "I think maybe some of us owe you an apology, Tim."

"First things first. Let's just get Germaine to the trauma center," said Tim. "I never took anything personally, Clem."

Flossie Fingerpie picked up Doozy Dorking and packed her under her arm. She coaxed Beatrice to climb up on her shoulder so they could trudge back to Fingerpie Farm. "Maybe your brother, Amos, was trying to get your attention," Flossie said to Beatrice. "Maybe he knew Miss Earth wasn't dinner material and would need to be rescued. And since he couldn't communicate with us, he found you. His sister. And his stepchicken, Doozy. His family. Even mutants can have families, you know. And families stick together in times of trouble."

"Sometimes," said Josif Mustard, looking fondly at his wife.

"Sometimes," said Grandma Earth, looking fondly at her daughter.

"Sometimes," said Thud Tweed, in a less rosy voice, looking at no one in particular. "Sometimes not."

Trooper Crawdad had already alerted Hamlet Rescue, and the crew was waiting with a stretcher. As soon as Miss Earth was ready, they bundled her up the hill as fast as they could climb. Timothy Grass kept pace with the crew and held Miss Earth's hand. Her eyes were bright with hope and pleasure at finding herself alive, and from time to time her hand twitched, as if the nerves were waking.

All her students ran along after her. Several of them were sobbing with relief. And not all of those were girls. Salim's eyes were wet, and Thud's were too.

For the time being, a few townspeople stayed behind to keep an eye on the second cocoon, Norma Jean and Josif Mustard, Mr. Grubb, and Mrs. Bannerjee among them. The town would have to work out a system of vigilance. Whatever might hatch from this cocoon was going to be too large to hide in the woods, and better safe than sorry, this time.

Clem Fawcett stayed there too. "Whatever it is, it's up to no good," he declared. "Happy endings don't make any sense in this neck of the woods. Not when you're dealing with giant mutant chickens."

A couple of days later, Thekla Mustard met Thud Tweed at Clumpett's General Store.

"Do you know how Miss Earth is doing?" she asked him.

"I'm not staying at the Earths' house anymore," he said, sounding a little disappointed. "Harold came back from his trip, and besides, Grandma Earth had a lot of nursing to do. But I do stop by and help with the doughnuts," he added.

"Your first job," she said. "You get paid?"

"Not in cash."

"Oh. Doughnuts?"

He shook his head. Thekla didn't ask any more. She thought she knew the answer. Thud got paid in something more important than money *or* doughnuts. It was—what? Being needed. Being thought responsible. Something like that.

Thud was a big kid, and Miss Earth's other students were still a little in awe of him. He was growing up bigger and maybe faster than they were. Just the way Amos had grown up bigger and faster than Beatrice. But Amos and Beatrice were still related. They were the same species—the only two Flameburpers there were. Thekla was more and more convinced that Amos had been skulking around Fingerpie Farm to attract Beatrice's attention, to let her know she wasn't the last of her kind in the universe. It wasn't necessarily good or bad, just common survival, not wanting to feel alone.

So Thud didn't feel alone, helping out at Grandma Earth's Baked Goods and Auto Repair Shop. Good for him. And Thekla felt a little less alone too. She was back in command at the head of the Tattletales. She still had to find a way to make it up to Mayor Grass, but that very impulse seemed to her a grown-up sort of sensation. So she was a bit closer to her older father and her eager mother than she had been a few weeks earlier.

It was a good feeling, to imagine oneself just a bit more grown up than before. Maybe not as thrilling as, oh, say, total world domination. But nice enough in its own right.

Mrs. Mustard stayed on as substitute teacher for another three weeks or so. Dr. Sternbaum prohibited Miss Earth from returning to work until May first.

Before Miss Earth returned, she wrote an open letter to all Hamlet citizens. It was published in the *Hamlet Holler*. In it she thanked everyone for their kindness and expressed regret for the trouble she'd caused.

She was careful to write obliquely about her ordeal so as not to put in print any specific mention of the Flameburper. Miss Earth said that she had gone for a walk, slipped on a muddy bit, and knocked her head on a boulder. Perhaps she'd been bitten by a creature and slipped into a coma; at any rate, it was a miracle that she hadn't suffered debilitating frostbite or worse. The happy works of Nature had kept her warm and dry until she could be discovered. For that she was grateful, and she would also be grateful not to discuss the matter again, since she wanted to get back to teaching and focus on more important matters like the education of children.

As it happened, the day she returned to work, the Science Fair opened in the auditorium.

It was the best Science Fair you ever saw. The kindergartners had gotten bored with growing grass in milk cartons and had grown miniature rainforests instead, complete with plastic gorillas in the ivy and fake rain made from leftover Christmas tinsel.

The lower school brought in pets and stuffed animals. Some of the stuffed animals scared the pets. It is possible some of the pets scared the stuffed animals too.

Miss Earth's class had done exemplary work. The students had borrowed from the kindergarten the Wheel of Life poster and pinned it to an easel, and in the middle of the easel they had pasted a huge question mark.

Beyond the easel stood eight folding card tables arranged in a circle. They displayed your standard-issue student projects. Placards of white cardboard with hand-lettered titles, or computer-generated text in as many colors as the printer could manage. There were drawings and photos, graphs and charts. Each separate display included a list of Books for Further Learning that no one would ever use.

But the best part of the display, said Miss Earth, was the concept of it.

The tables had been set up more or less in a circle. Along the edges of the tables, the children had taped paper with huge printed words on it. If you stood in the middle and rotated, you could read what it said.

On the table tops were pictures of microbes, fleas, mice, cats, dogs, wolves, bears, and human beings. Predators and prey.

Along the edges of the table, the other opinion of Miss Earth's class:

PREDATORS
AND
PREY?
TOGETHER
IN
PEACE?
YOU
CHOOSE!

Miss Earth thought it was dubious that a cat could choose not to prey on a mouse, or a microbe decide not to infect the intestine of a wolf. But sometimes being a good teacher meant keeping your mouth shut. If her students were learning to choose, that was lesson enough.

"I love it," she said. "Well done, class. You've considered the subject, you've worked in pairs, and together you've shaped it into a single message. Bravo, one and all."

"I see that Pearl Hotchkiss displayed a picture of herself as an example of a human being," said Sammy Grubb to Thekla Mustard. "Good thing we were assigned bears; you couldn't have pictured yourself as a human being. I don't think you qualify."

"For once I agree with you," said Thekla Mustard. "I'm working at becoming a minor deity. It's time to set my sights a little higher."

"A minor deity is just another kind of Missing Link," said Sammy Grubb.

"A minor deity is better than a major celebrity," said Lois Kennedy the Third, listening in. "Look at Thud's mom, back from her tour."

Mrs. Mildred Tweed had come straight from the airport for the opening of the Science Fair. She hadn't had time to change out of her Petunia Whiner garb, and her ten-gallon Stetson was wobbling on top of her twelve gallons of hair. "Thud, this is a work of genius!" she was gushing. "Who knew you had academic talent?"

"Glad you're home, Momster," said Thud. And he was. But she looked like an example of a human specimen gone mutant herself. "Could you, like—go *home*? And change?"

"We all change, sooner or later," said Mrs. Tweed. "You're changing too, Thud. You're becoming a student. And—I do believe you're growing up."

"I've been grown up since I was five and a half, Mom," said Thud.

"You are big for your age, always were," she replied. "I mean growing up inside."

"Well," he said, "think of the teachers I've had!"

He looked around the room. Miss Earth was still inspecting the displays. Principal Buttle, Jasper Stripe, Mayor Grass, Mrs. Brill, and Mrs. Cobble were looking on warmly. Other parents—Dr. Mustard, the Bannerjees, Stan's mom and her friend, the Petroses, the Reverend Mrs. Mopp—were examining the displays with pride too. Townspeople like the Clumpetts, and Clem Fawcett, and the Fingerpies, even though they had no kids in school now, were there to beam and admire and learn about Science.

The whole clot and collection of them were teachers, in a way.

Mrs. Mustard wasn't there, though. She was busy at her next teaching assignment.

Black fly season still hadn't begun, thank goodness. So she sat in the woods, hour after hour, on a folding camp chair. She read aloud to the creature in the cocoon. She read *Just So Stories;* she read Mother Goose rhymes; she read "The Lady or the Tiger?" over and over again.

"Remember what my mother-in-law used to say," she lectured the silent creature inside. "Life is short, and everything you do counts. Beware what you choose. What'll it be? Eeny, meeny, miney, moe. Catch a mutant by the toe. What will you choose? How will you grow? Eeny, meeny, miney, moe."

The cocoon gave off a gentle breath of warm smell from time to time, like the first faintly smoking charcoal briquettes of the summer season.

"April may be the season for April fools," said Mrs. Mustard, "but April showers bring May flowers." She felt like a woodland flower herself, blossoming again after a long winter's sleep.